THIS BOOK BELONGS TO

Dear Ramsay and Naya,

We hope you love Steve and Eve!

Deborah + Paul

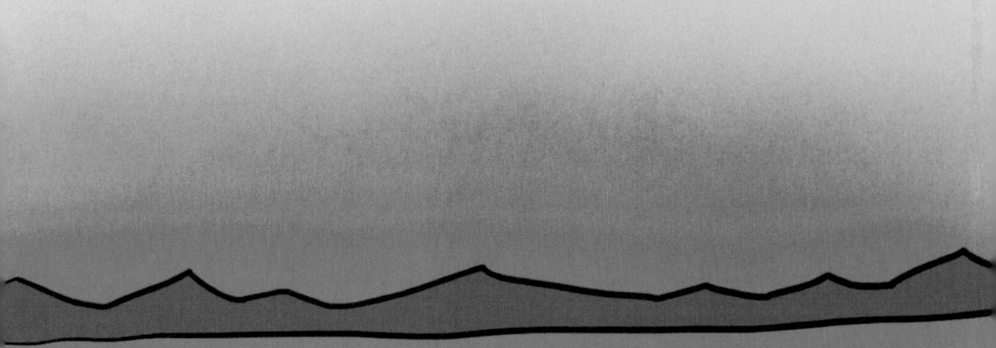

This book was created with love and appreciation for the land, peoples, and cultures across the country whereupon this project was envisioned or depicted, including the traditional territories of the Inuit Nunangat, Musqueam, Tsleil-Waututh, S'ólh Téméxw, Hul'qumi'num, Stz'uminus, Cayuse, Umatilla, Walla Walla, Lil'wat, Squamish, St'at'imc, Tla'amin, Homalco, Klahoose, Anishinabewaki, Wendake-Nionwentsïo, Haudenosaunee, and Mississauga nations.

We recognize all First Nations, Métis and Inuit Peoples who are the original caretakers of the lands currently called Canada. Their deep connection and relationship to these lands, and the Indigenous Knowledge they continue to pass down through story and song, continue to inspire and guide us. We honour the Knowledge Keepers and Elders who give voice to the land and animals who sustain us all.

STEVE AND EVE

SAVE THE PLANET

I CAN HEAR YOUR HEART BEEP

Written by
Paul Shore & Deborah Katz Henriquez

Illustrated by
Prashant Miranda

PLANET HERO KIDS

www.PlanetHeroKids.com

Published by Planet Hero Kids, Vancouver, BC

Cataloguing data available from Library and Archives Canada
ISBN 978-0-9813474-4-8 (hardcover)
ISBN 978-0-9813474-5-5 (paperback)
ISBN 978-0-9813474-6-2 (ebook)

1 2 3 4 5 6 7 8 9 10

First edition, February 2023

Edited by David Adams
Cover design by John Ngan and Soumya of Henriquez Partners Architects
Book design by Prashant Miranda and Henriquez Partners Architects

For my mother Zelda, whose love and kindness lives on in the soul of this story and in every person who she touched. And thank you, Jashia and Aaron, for all your playful ideas and teaching me to listen more carefully to kids, who just seem to know what's healthy for the planet.
Paul

For my father Harold, whose humor and gentle nature live on in this story and in our hearts, for my children – you inspire me everyday with your insight, creativity, and curiosity, and to Gregory, for your unwavering love, steadfast devotion, and support.
Deborah

To my ancestors and
for my parents John & Majella Miranda,
who continue to teach me in exemplary ways.
Prashant

Thank you to our friends with PhDs in Curiosity: David Adams for magically teasing the best story possible out of us and Charles Holmes for continuously encouraging us to make ripples. Thank you to Joan Richoz, Joyce Pagurek, and Susan Katz for keeping our language and spelling tidy; to Joel Solomon for encouraging so many fine humans to pursue a Hollyhock education to help release their creativity to the world; to electric car champion Kyle Lockhart for saving the "best-email-ever"; to Charlie Latimer for making the most important introduction ever; to Catherine Kargas, a beloved and inspiring figure in the zero-emission transportation community; and to Henriquez Partners Architects for their generous and talented graphic design services and support. Plus a special thank you to the universe and all our friends and families for supplying big buckets of support and serendipity.

And one last bear hug and thank you to all the
Save The Planet Heroes out there,
who are spreading kindness, like jam on toast!

Paul, Deborah, Prash, Steve, and Eve.

CHAPTERS

CHAPTER 1

FISHTACHIO BANDITS

MART

FREEZER

FISHTACHIO ICE CREAM,
YESSS!
GRAB AS MANY BUCKETS
AS YOU CAN STEVE!

SAMI, ARE YOU SURE
ABOUT THIS?

AREN'T YOU HUNGRY?
THERE ARE HARDLY
ANY FISH IN
THE OCEAN
TO EAT!
WELL, YEAH THAT'S TRUE, BUT...

THEN CATCH!
FREEZER

BUT SAMI, IT
JUST DOESN'T
FEEL RIGHT...

STEVE-O! HOW OFTEN DOES THAT
BIG SHIP COME TO FILL UP
OUR GROCERY STORES?

I THINK IT'S JUST ONCE A YEAR...
BUT...

CORRRRRECT MY POLAR PAL!
AND WHY IS THAT?

UMMM, CUZ THE GINORMOUS SHIP CAN ONLY COME IN THE SUMMER, WHEN THE SEA ICE ISN'T SO THICK... BUT...
MART

SO, HOW MANY TIMES A YEAR CAN HUNGRY FRIENDS STOCK UP ON FISHTACHIO ICE CREAM?

SO, HOW MANY DAYS BEFORE WE CAN STOCK UP AGAIN IF WE DON'T CATCH ENOUGH FISH TO EAT THIS YEAR?

WELL, THERE ARE 365 DAYS IN A YEAR, SO IF YOU SUBTRACT 1 FROM 365, THAT MAKES 364 DAYS UNTIL THIS SHIP COMES HERE AGAIN, BUT...

CORRRRRECT AGAIN! KEEP ON CATCHIN' AND STACKIN'!

BUT SAMI, I JUST DON'T THINK THAT WE SHOULD BE...

BOO

NOT FUNNY WHISKERS! I NEARLY LOST A TOE!

SORRY STEVE!
WOW, LOOK AT ALL THAT FISHTACHIO ICE CREAM! YOU REALLY HIT THE JACKPOT!

SHHHHHHH....
SOMEBODY IS GOING TO HEAR US, AND WE REALLY SHOULDN'T BE...

COME ON STEVE, WE'RE JUST TAKING A FEW FISHY SNACKS!

BESIDES, THE FISH IN THIS ICE CREAM SHOULD STILL BE IN THE OCEAN FOR US!

YEAH, BUT...

SAMI, YOU KNOW I SWORE OFF EATING MAMMALS AFTER YOU SAVED MY LIFE WHEN I WAS A CUB!

NO, NO, NO!

WHAT AM I DOING?!
LET'S PUT ALL THIS BACK
AND TRY TO CATCH FISH
ON OUR OWN, OK?

UH OH, I THINK THE GIG IS UP --
I HEAR DOGS!

RUN!

AND DON'T LEAVE THE SLED OF
GOODIES BEHIND!

STEVE, MEET ME AT THE SECRET HIDING SPOT!
SAMI, WE ARE IN BIG TROUBLE!

RUN, STEVE, RUN!

WHOLLY FROZEN PENGUIN TOOTS, THEY'RE SHOOTING ***HARE*** BALLS AT ME!

I GUESS HUMANS REALLY LIKE THEIR ICE CREAM!

...

I NEVER SHOULD HAVE EATEN THAT WHOLE BOX OF CRAB CUPCAKES FOR BREAKFAST!

AWWWWW, THOSE SKINNY DOGS ARE PROBABLY AS HUNGRY AS I AM... POOR LITTLE DOGGIES!

HERE YOU GO DOGGIES -- HAVE SOME ICE CREAM!
SORRY THAT SAMI AND I TOOK IT -- WE WERE JUST SUPER HUNGRY!

DON'T EAT TOO FAST DOGGIES, OR YOU'LL GET BRAIN FREEZE!

HOW DID THINGS EVER GET THIS BAD?
HA HA HA!
NO, NO, NOT MY ARMPITS, ZEL -- YOU KNOW I'M SUPER TICKLISH THERE!

YOU TICKLE-WRESTLERS ARE MISSING OUT ON SALMON BURGERS AND KELP CHIPS. COME AND GET SOME BEFORE HAL SCARFS THEM ALL DOWN!

MMMMMM, DO YOU SMELL THOSE BURGERS!? TIME OUT FROM WRESTLING -- LET'S GO EAT!

EAT UP EVERYONE! IT WARMS MY HEART TO WATCH YOU LITTLE MUNCHKINS EAT.
DO YOU KNOW HOW MUCH YOUR DAD AND I LOVE YOU CUBS?

HOW MUCH?!
THIS MUCH! MORE THAN ALL THE ICE IN THE ARCTIC!

LOOK AT
GRANDPA HARRY --
WOW, CAN HE
EVER EAT!
DON'T LOOK NOW BUT
HERE COMES MY
FAVORITE PART
OF DINNER.
GRANDPA HARRY IS
ABOUT TO FINISH
HIS PIE AND DRINK HIS
BERRY JUICE!
WAIT FOR IT...

THAT WAS A STINKY ONE --
I THINK I SMELL HERRING!

YES -- WITH A HINT OF
SALMON AND BERRIES --
EEEEEWWW!

MOM SAYS "TO-PIE-YUM" MEANS
SOMETHING LIKE "TO LIFE" OR
"CHEERS", RIGHT?

WHATEVER IT MEANS, IT GOES WELL WITH A HUMONGOUS SMELLY BELCH!
HA HA HA!

MY TURN, MY TURN -- DON'T FORGET MY NOSE KISS MOMMY!
HEY, THERE YOU ARE! I THOUGHT THEY CAUGHT YOU! HOW LONG HAVE YOU BEEN HERE?

OH... UMMMM... NOT VERY LONG.
SORRY, BUT I LOST ALMOST ALL
THE BUCKETS OF ICE CREAM
ALONG THE WAY.

DON'T WORRY ABOUT IT.
COME INSIDE PAL,
YOU LOOK TIRED!

WHAT?!?!
YOU LIVE LIKE THE KING OF THE SEA!

IT'S NO PALACE, BUT I DO OK.

WHERE DID YOU GET ALL THIS ICE CREAM? THIS PLACE LOOKS LIKE YOU ROBBED A SVEN AND BARRY'S ICE CREAM FACTORY.

I HAVE SOME FRIENDS?...

BUT YOU TOLD ME I WAS YOUR ONLY HOPE TO LOAD UP ON ICE CREAM!

WELL, MAYBE I FIBBED JUST A LITTLE... AHEM.

SAAAMMMMI?!

OK, OK, SO I PRETTY MUCH HAD ALL YOUR SIBLINGS AND COUSINS -- AND OK, OK, PRETTY MUCH ANYONE ELSE I COULD FIND -- DO ICE CREAM RAIDS ON THE BIG SHIP IN THE HARBOR TOO.

SAMI!!

IT ONLY COMES ONCE A YEAR, STEVE! I HAD TO MAKE SURE WE STOCKED UP ENOUGH TO LAST TILL NEXT YEAR!

IT'S OK, SAMI, I FORGIVE YOU. HUNGER CAN MAKE A SEAL DO STRANGE THINGS -- LIKE BRINGING MY WHOLE FAMILY INTO A LIFE OF CRIME!

DID ZEL AND HAL AT LEAST GET ENOUGH TO EAT? I HAVEN'T SEEN THEM SINCE LAST WEEK WHEN WE GOT CHASED AWAY FROM THAT BEACH BARBECUE WE SNUCK INTO.

I COULD REALLY GO FOR ONE OF THOSE AMAZING BARNACLE BURGERS RIGHT NOW -- DRIPPING WITH JUICY JELLYFISH JAM!...

WELL, THERE ARE NO BURGERS HERE MY FRIEND -- BUT WE'VE GOT FISHTACHIO ICE CREAM BY THE BUCKET! GRAB A SPOON AND DIG IN, PAL!

NO THANKS, MAYBE LATER, SAMI. I'M NOT FEELING SO HUNGRY ANYMORE.

WHAT? YOU?

NOT HUNGRY?

WHAT GIVES STEVE?

I DON'T KNOW, SAMI. THIS IS JUST ALL WRONG. IT'S LIKE THE PLANET'S BROKEN OR SOMETHING! THERE'S NO FOOD FOR US IN THE OCEAN SO WE HAVE TO TAKE IT FROM THE STORE, AND ON TOP OF THAT, MY PARENTS WENT AWAY TO FIND FOOD AND THEY HAVEN'T COME BACK. I'M GETTING WORRIED ABOUT THEM! IT'S NOT SUPPOSED TO BE LIKE THIS.

AND LOOK AT YOU -- YOU'RE SUPPOSED TO BE SWIMMING AND CATCHING FISH IN THE OCEAN, PLAYING WITH THE OTHER SEALS -- NOT STOCKPILING BUCKETS OF ICE CREAM IN AN IGLOO!

AWW, CHEER UP STEVE, IT'S NOT SO BAD. AT LEAST WE HAVE SOMETHING TO PUT IN OUR HUNGRY BELLIES! HERE -- I MADE A WAFFLE CONE FOR YOU -- HAVE SOME ICE CREAM AND YOU'LL FEEL BETTER.

AND AS IF I DIDN'T HAVE ENOUGH PROBLEMS -- WHY DO I HAVE SUCH WEIRD-LOOKING PAWS?

FUNNY-LOOKING PAWS FOR A BEAR! WHERE'S THE LEPRECHAUN THAT GOES WITH THOSE RAINBOWS? HAAAAA HAAAA!

STRANGE PAWS, FELLA! I CAN SEE YOU COMING A MILE AWAY WITH THOSE GLOW-IN-THE-DARK GLOVES YOU GOT THERE! I'M LOOKIN' FOR LOVE, BUT ALL I KEEP FINDING IS YOU!

OH DANCING LIGHTS,
PLEASE HELP!

CHAPTER 2

MAKE LIKE A TREE AND LEAF

FLYING WITH THE BIRDS, GROOVING TO MY TUNES... LIFE IS AWESOME!
BIRDS FLYING HIGH, YOU KNOW HOW I FEEL, SUN IN THE SKY, YOU KNOW HOW I FEEL, BREEZE DRIFTIN' ON BY, YOU KNOW HOW I FEEL...

HI THERE GEESE! ISN'T
IT GREAT UP HERE IN
THE FRESH AIR?
WAY BETTER THAN ON
THE GROUND WITH MY
GASSY CAR COUSINS!

HUMPH, I BET THEY'RE
LANDING FOR DINNER.
I'M HUNGRY TOO --
I NEED TO CHARGE UP!

OH NO, NOT YOU BULLIES AGAIN!
GO DRINK SOME DINOSAUR-JUICE
AND LEAVE ME ALONE!

THAT SHOWS HOW LITTLE YOU KNOW, YOU ELECTRICITY MUNCHER! WE DON'T DRINK DINOSAUR JUICE -- WE DRINK GAS!

GAS COMES FROM ANCIENT LIFE FORMS THAT ARE AS OLD AS DINOSAURS! NOT NEARLY AS FRESH AND TASTY AS MY ELECTRON LUNCH!

YOU THINK
YOU'RE SO
MUCH BETTER
THAN US,
MISS PERFECT!

STICKS AND STONES
MAY BREAK MY
BATTERIES, BUT
NAMES WILL NEVER
HURT ME!

YOU ARE ALL JUST SO MEAN AND PREHISTORIC! LEAVE ME ALONE!

HUH? PREHISTORIC? WHO CARES ABOUT HISTORY?

PREHISTORIC MEANS VERY, VERY, VERY, VERY, VERY OLD.

HUH? WE'RE NOT EVEN TEN YEARS OLD! WHO ARE YOU CALLING OLD?!

YOU DRINK GAS, WHICH COMES FROM OIL, WHICH COMES FROM PREHISTORIC CREATURES!

AND DRINKING THAT DINOSAUR JUICE GIVES YOU SMELLY TOOTS THAT TURN INTO SMOG!

WHAT? WE'RE PROUD OF OUR STINKY TOOTS! AND THEY AREN'T CAUSING SMOG -- THAT'S CAUSED BY BURPING BULLFROGS!

WHAT?! DID YOU JUST MAKE THAT UP, MR. FAKER BAKER?

YEP!

WELL, I BELIEVE IN *SCIENCE*, NOT NONSENSE!

IF YOU DON'T LIKE WHAT I HAVE TO SAY, YOU SHOULD GO FIND YOUR OWN KIND -- LIKE MAYBE A FAMILY OF ELECTRIC TOASTERS!
HA HA HA!
HA HA!
HA HA
SCRAM, SKEDADDLE! MAKE LIKE A TREE AND LEAF!
THAT'S THE ONLY CLEVER THING YOU'VE SAID -- I'M OUTTA HERE!

YOU'RE METAL AND GLASS JUST LIKE US -- BUT YOU THINK YOU'RE SO SPECIAL WITH YOUR ELECTRIC MOTOR AND FANCY COMPUTER.

I **AM** SPECIAL! AND DON'T FORGET MY WINGS OF AWESOMENESS!

YOU'RE JUST A HEARTLESS MACHINE, SISTER -- LIKE US -- YOU'LL NEVER MAKE A DIFFERENCE IN THIS WORLD!

OH YEAH? I WILL SO MAKE A DIFFERENCE -- YOU'LL SEE!

OUCH! I'LL REMEMBER THAT DENT AS A BADGE OF HONOR -- I'M LEAVING THIS PLACE TO FIND MY PACK -- MY KIND -- REAL FRIENDS -- WHO WILL UNDERSTAND ME!

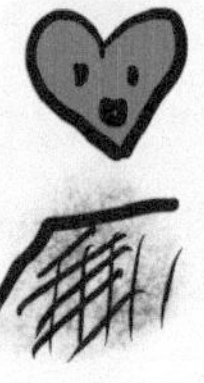

OH YEAH, WHAT PACK IS THAT, MS. FANCY PANTS?

ELCIHEV CIRTCELE.
IT SAYS SO ON MY BUMPER STICKER.

ACTUALLY, BEFORE I GO, I JUST WANT TO SAY THAT YOUR ANCESTORS WERE ACTUALLY GOOD FOLKS. WHEN CARS WERE INVENTED THEY MADE A REAL DIFFERENCE IN THE WORLD. BUT NOW WE REALIZE THAT ALL THE GAS YOU BURN IS HURTING THE PLANET -- SO IT'S TIME TO CHANGE.

CHAPTER 3

ACCIDENTAL TOURIST

I'M DONE WITH THOSE DINOSAUR-JUICE-DRINKING MEANIES! I NEED TO FIND MY PACK -- THE YIN TO MY CLANG, THE CHEESE TO MY MACARONI. WHERE SHOULD I LOOK FIRST?

COMPUTER, PLEASE BOOGLE

"ELCIHEV CIRTCELE".

Sorry, no results found for "Elcihev Cirtcele".

HMMM... THAT'S STRANGE! MAYBE I HAVE TO START WITH THE BASICS. COMPUTER, PLEASE BOOGLE WHERE I CAN FIND THE MOST ELECTRIC VEHICLES IN THE WORLD.

NORWAY NORWAY NORWAY. Most new cars in Norway are electric!

YIPPEE! NORWAY, HERE I COME!

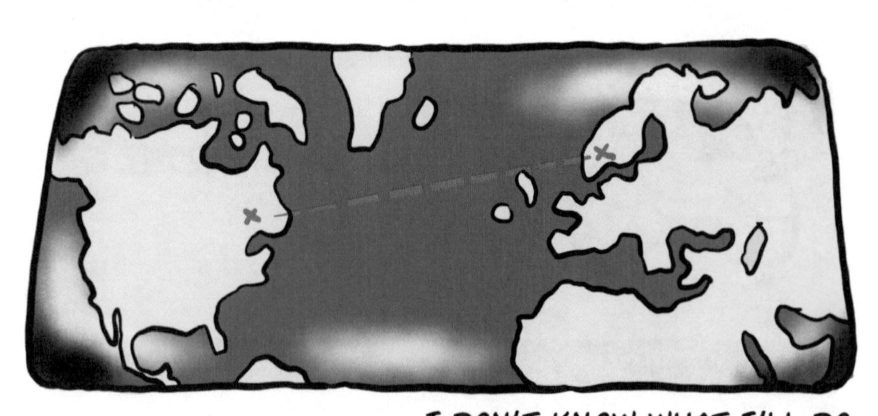

I DON'T KNOW WHAT I'LL DO ONCE I FIND MY PACK, BUT I CAN FEEL IT IN MY BATTERIES THAT WE ARE GOING TO DO SOME SHOCKINGLY COOL STUFF TOGETHER! TIME TO ACTIVATE SUPERMEGASONIC SPEED AND GET TO NORWAY FAST!

SUPERMEGASONIC SPEED TO NORWAY

AHHHHHH... THE COOL AIR ON MY WINDSHIELD. WEEEEEE... SOARING THROUGH PILLOWS OF ICE CRYSTALS FLOATING IN THE SKY!

ZZZZZZZZZOOOOOOOOM ARAMA... SUPERMEGASONIC SPEED! ZOWWWWIE! THE OCEAN IS SO AWESOMELY HUGE AND SO AWESOMELY BLUE -- I SEE AWESOMENESS EVERYWHERE!!!

CANADA
NORWAY

IT'S A NEW DAWN, IT'S A NEW DAY, IT'S A NEW LIFE, FOR ME...
AND I'M FEELING GOOD, I'M FEELING GOOD.

WELL BUTTER MY BUMPER! THIS FOG IS THICKER THAN VANILLA PUDDING! I BET IF I TURN ON MY HIGH-VOLTAGE BEAMS, I CAN ZAP THE FOG AND BE IN NORWAY BY 9 O'CLOCK TONIGHT!

Caution!
POLAR BEAR
Crossing
Ahead!

POLAR BEAR CROSSING? HOLY SMOKING ELECTRONS! I DIDN'T EVEN KNOW THERE WERE POLAR BEARS IN NORWAY! MAYBE I CAN SPOT ONE IF I SWOOP DOWN JUST A LITTLE!

FUNNY, I DIDN'T THINK I WOULD GET TO NORWAY SO QUICKLY. I EVEN IMPRESS MYSELF SOMETIMES! -- EVE THE WONDER CAR, EVE THE MAGNIFICENT, EVE THE...

WHAT IN THE BEEEEEEEEEEEEEEP???

...... WHAT'S GOING ON! I BETTER ACTIVATE LANDING MODE!

OUCHA WOUCHA ZOUCHA!
THAT'S GONNA LEAVE A MARK! WHERE AM I?...
I CAN'T SEE ANYTHING BUT WHITE!

WHAT KIND OF WEIRD
FOG IS THIS?!
AND WHY IS MY FACE
SO FRIGIDLY FROZEN?

WHAT IN THE
BEEEEEPPPP?!
EVEN MY WIPERS
DON'T WORK!

AND MY WHEELS WON'T MOVE!
THERE COULD BE WILD ANIMALS
AROUND HERE... **YIKES!!**

mmmmph

B-E-E-E-E-E-E-P! PLEASE LET GO OF ME! DON'T HURT ME!

HEY! STOP
QUIRMING AND
EAMING, YOU ICY
UE CREATURE!
'RE FROZEN! I'M
NG TO HELP YOU!

KE SHAKE!
SHAKE!

PHEW!

SWIM SO WILD,
B·E·E·P

SOMETHING IS SINGING!
HEY,
H --E --L --L --P!
B --E --E --E --P!

AND YOU SWIM SO FREE.

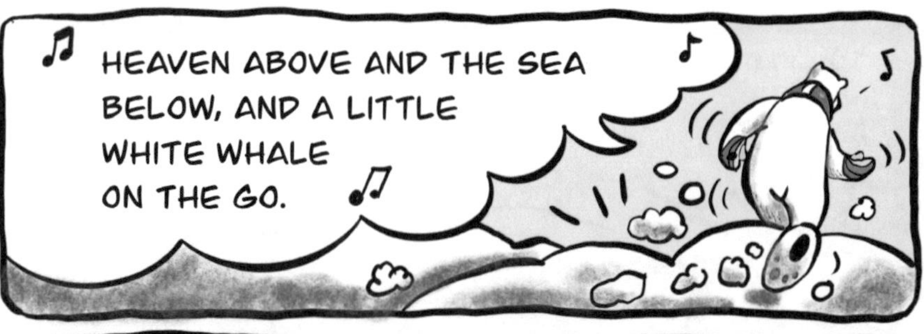

CHAPTER 4

GRILLED FISH

DON'T BE AFRAID! I DON'T BITE -- UNLESS YOU'RE A FISH OF COURSE!

CAN YOU PLEASE WIPE MY EYES?
SURE, BUT WHERE ARE YOUR EYES?

ON MY HOOD! DON'T YOU SEE THEM?

WOW! YOU'RE A BEAR! BUT YOU SURE ARE ONE STRANGE ISBJØRN! YOUR PAWS LOOK LIKE THEY'VE BEEN DIPPED IN COTTON CANDY!

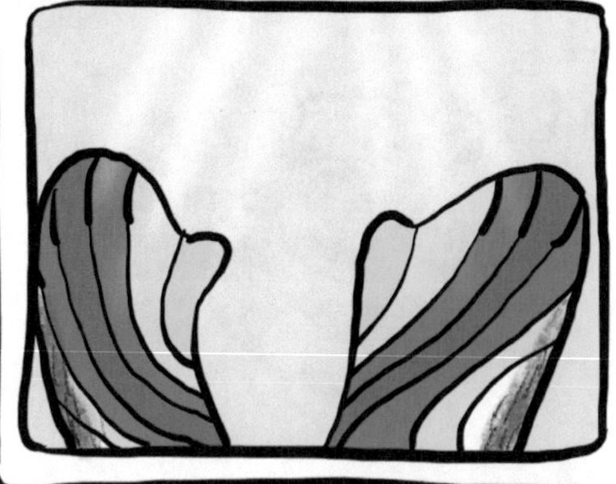

I KNOW, I KNOW - MY PAWS ARE KINDA STRANGE LOOKING, BUT I'VE NEVER BEEN CALLED AN ISBJØRN BEFORE! MY NAME IS STEVE, AND YOU'VE GOT IT RIGHT THAT I'M A BEAR -- BUT I'M A POLAR BEAR. P-O-L-A-R -- ***POLAR*** -- AS IN, THE NORTH POLE!

WHAT?! I'M NOT IN NORWAY? I'M AT THE NORTH POLE?!

WELL, ALMOST -- WE'RE JUST OUTSIDE OF A TOWN THE HUMANS CALL EEE-CAAA--LOOW--IT.

THEY SAY IT MEANS "PLACE OF MANY FISH", THOUGH THESE DAYS IT FEELS MORE LIKE THERE ARE NO DRIPPIN-FLIPPIN FISH!

WHOA -- EASY BIG FELLA! IT SOUNDS LIKE YOU'RE HUNGRY!

HUNGRY? YES -- VERY, VERY HUNGRY! BUT WHAT WERE YOU SAYING ABOUT NORWAY? NEVER HEARD OF THAT PLACE BEFORE -- IS THAT WHERE YOU WERE HEADING?

YES, I HAD SET MY NAVIGATION SYSTEM TO NORWAY, SO I THOUGHT THAT'S WHERE I LANDED -- SOMETHING MUST'VE GONE TERRIBLY WRONG WITH MY ONBOARD COMPUTER! AND ISBJØRN IS THE WORD THEY USE IN NORWAY FOR POLAR BEAR. 'IS' MEANS 'ICE" AND 'BJØRN' MEANS 'BEAR'. "ICE BEAR", GET IT? WHEN I SAW YOU, I THOUGHT YOU WERE A NORWEGIAN ISBJØRN!

SO YOU'RE A LANGUAGE TEACHER THAT FELL OUT OF THE SKY, WHO SPEAKS POLAR BEAR?!

YOU ARE A *FUNNY* ISBJØRN! BUT WHAT'S WITH YOUR PAWS? -- SINCE WHEN DO POLAR BEARS HAVE PAWS LIKE RAINBOWS?

SINCE I WAS BORN WITH THEM THIS WAY! I KNOW THEY'RE REALLY WEIRD -- THANKS FOR POINTING THAT OUT! AT LEAST YOU DIDN'T LAUGH AT ME LIKE SOME OF THE OTHER ANIMALS DO.

SORRY, STEVE! HEY -- BEING DIFFERENT IS SPECIAL -- IT'S **AWESOME,** ACTUALLY! I THINK YOUR PAWS MAKE YOU RARE -- WHICH MAKES YOU AN **AWESOME RARE BEAR!** THOUGH YOU SEEM AWFULLY KIND FOR A BEAR -- I THOUGHT BEARS WERE SUPPOSED TO BE SCARY!
AWW GEESH, THANKS! YOU SEEM NICE TOO. AND ABOUT MY PAWS -- THE STRANGE THING IS THAT SOMETIMES THEY TURN ALL WHITE FOR NO REASON -- LIKE A REGULAR BEAR. I HAVE NO IDEA WHY, OR WHEN IT'S GOING TO HAPPEN -- IT JUST DOES! BUT THEN THEY GO BACK TO BEING COLORFUL.

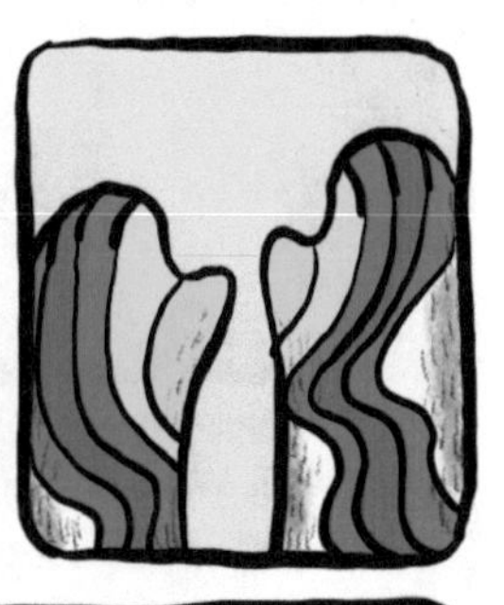
THEY SURE HAVE A MIND OF THEIR OWN!

WOW -- THAT'S INCREDIBLE! I DON'T CARE WHAT THE OTHER ANIMALS SAY -- I THINK THAT THEY ARE VERY "HAND-SOME"!

VERY FUNNY. THANKS FOR SAYING THAT. I JUST WISH THEY WOULD STAY WHITE FOREVER, BUT NO MATTER HOW HARD I WISH, THEY ALWAYS TURN BACK TO THIS!

WELL, I BOW TO THE AMAZINGNESS OF YOUR MOST RARE-OSITY.

THANKS! THAT'S THE NICEST THING ANYBODY HAS EVER SAID TO ME!

NAMASTE, MY NEW FRIEND, NAMASTE.

WHAT'S A NAAAMAAASTAY MISS LANGUAGE TEACHER?

OH, IT MEANS "THE DIVINE IN ME, BOWS TO THE DIVINE IN YOU".
SAY WHHAAAAT?

OH, ANOTHER WAY TO SAY THAT IS "WHAT IS SPECIAL IN ME, RESPECTS WHAT IS SPECIAL IN YOU".

WOW -- THAT'S COOL. NAMASTE TO YOU, UMMM, WHAT'S YOUR NAME?
EVE!

I'VE NEVER SEEN ANYTHING LIKE YOU BEFORE! ARE YOU SOME KIND OF SPACE BEAR SENT TO EARTH TO TEACH ME COOL WORDS?

ARE THESE YOUR EARS?

AND IS THIS YOUR MOUTH?
THIS MUST BE YOUR MOUTH.
WAIT HERE -- I'LL BE
RIGHT BACK!

WHAT IN THE WORLD ARE YOU DOING? STOP THAT!

I THOUGHT YOU MIGHT BE HUNGRY AFTER BEING FROZEN, SO I'M SHARING! THESE ARE THE LAST TWO DELICIOUS FISH THAT I STASHED UNDER A ROCK LAST WEEK. ONE FOR YOU... ONE FOR ME!

EEEWWW, GROSSSSSSS!... PLEASE STOP TRYING TO FEED THAT SALVELINUS ALPINUS AND BOREOGADUS SAIDA TO ME!

?
THAT BORING SAID A WHAAAAAT? I'M FEEDING YOU DELICICOUS **FISH!!!**

OH, THOSE ARE THE SCIENTIFIC NAMES FOR ARCTIC CHAR AND ARCTIC COD, PAL.

WOULD FISHTACHIO ICE CREAM BE BETTER? THAT'S MY FAVORITE FOOD IN THE WHOLE WIDE WORLD!
AH, NO THANK YOU! I'M NOT A BEAR AND I DON'T EAT FISH OR ICE CREAM. I'M AN ELECTRIC CAR!

ELECTRIC CAR?... WHAT IN THE BELUGA IS THAT?
I'M A CAR AND I RUN 100% ON ELECTRICITY. I HAVE A COMPUTER TOO AND CAN LOOK UP JUST ABOUT ANYTHING YOU'D LIKE TO KNOW.

I THOUGHT CARS EAT SMELLY GAS THAT CATCHES ON FIRE IF YOU LIGHT A MATCH NEAR IT! ...
TOOT
BOOM

NO CAR THAT I EVER SAW
EATS ELECTRICITY.
HOW DO YOU EVEN DO THAT?!
DOESN'T THAT HURT?
BZZZT

HEY, IF YOU WOULD STOP DAY DREAMING AND SLOBBERING FISH PARTS FOR A SECOND, I CAN EXPLAIN!

OK, I'M ALL EARS! RIGHT AFTER I EAT THAT ARCTIC CAR FISH, SINCE YOU'RE NOT GOING TO!

GULP!
I THINK YOU MEAN ARCTIC **CHAR** FISH...!
HA HA

STEVE'S BEAR NECESSITIES

A Polar Bear's skin is black.

Sometimes Polar Bears and Grizzly Bears make babies together, called 'Grolar Bears' or 'Pizzly Bears'.

Polar Bears have scent glands in their paws, and it is believed that polar bears can communicate with each other through scent trails left by their paws on the ice.

When Polar Bears want to play fight they wag their heads from side to side and stand on their back legs.

CHAPTER 5

SMOKE AND MIRRORS

SO AS I WAS SAYING, I COME FROM A PLACE CALLED OSHAWA -- IT'S NEAR A HUGE CITY CALLED HOGTOWN.

YOU COME FROM A CITY OF PIGS? WOW!

THAT'S JUST A NICKNAME. HEY, WOULD YOU LISTEN AND STOP LICKING FISH BITS!

I CAN LISTEN AND LICK FISH BITS AT THE SAME TIME! YOU NEVER HEARD OF MULTITASKING?

I DIDN'T FEEL LIKE I FIT IN THERE, SO I SET OUT ON AN ADVENTURE LOOKING FOR MY PACK.

COOL - WHAT PACK ARE YOU FROM?

ELCIHEV CIRTCELE
ELCIHEV CIRTCELE. IT SAYS SO ON MY BUMPER STICKER, WHICH I CAN SEE IF I REACH MY MIRROR AROUND LIKE THIS...

I ASKED EVERY BIRD I FLEW PAST IF THEY COULD HELP ME FIND OTHERS FROM **ELCIHEV CIRTCELE,** BUT NO ONE HAD A CLUE!
UMM, EVE, I THINK I SEE YOUR PROBLEM.
MIRRORS MAKE WORDS APPEAR BACKWARDS -- YOUR BUMPER STICKER SAYS ELECTRIC VEHICLE, NOT **ELCHIHEV CIRTCELE!**

AWH-SUM
ELECTRIC VEHICLE

OH! THAT MAKES MUCH MORE SENSE! I AM AN ELECTRIC VEHICLE, OR E.V. FOR SHORT. THAT'S WHY THEY CALL ME "EVE"!

EVE THE E.V. CUTE!

THANKS --
BUT IF **ELCHIHEV CIRTCELE** REALLY JUST MEANS ELECTRIC VEHICLE, THEN WHAT IS THE NAME OF MY PACK?

I HAVE NO IDEA, PAL! LET'S PARK ALL THAT FOR A BIT! GET IT? PARK IT? HAHA! BY THE WAY, YOU ALSO HAVE A METAL THINGY ON YOUR BUM THAT SAYS AWH-SUM. WHAT'S WITH THAT?
HA HA!
AWH-SUM
ELECTRIC VEHICLE

THAT'S MY LICENSE PLATE! I CHOSE THOSE LETTERS CUZ THERE ARE SO MANY THINGS AROUND US THAT ARE AWESOME AND I LIKE TO REMIND MYSELF OF THAT ANY TIME I FEEL DOWN.

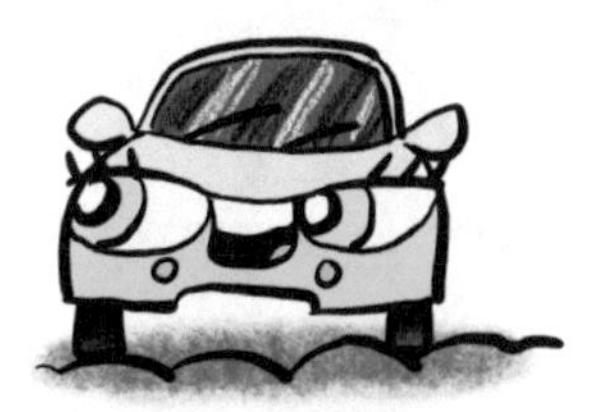

I LOVE IT! I COULD USE A DAILY REMINDER OF **AWESOME!**

YEAH, THERE'S ALWAYS SOMETHING AWESOME AROUND US. WE JUST NEED TO LOOK FOR IT! LIKE MY HOMETOWN OF OSHAWA IS **AWESOME,** ESPECIALLY BECAUSE BOBBY ORR IS FROM THERE.
BOBBY WHO?
AWH-SUM

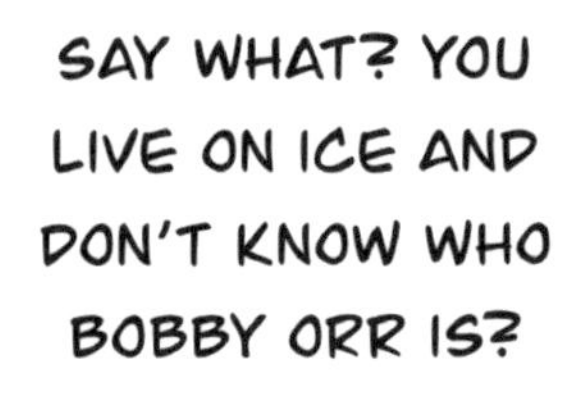

SAY WHAT? YOU LIVE ON ICE AND DON'T KNOW WHO BOBBY ORR IS?

NOPE AND WHAT'S ICE GOT TO DO WITH THAT?

BOBBY ORR IS ONE OF THE GREATEST HOCKEY PLAYERS WHO EVER LIVED!

WELL EXCUUUUUUUSE ME FOR NOT KNOWING THAT FACTOID. DO YOU SEE A LOT OF POLAR BEARS PLAYING HOCKEY?

WHAT WERE YOU SAYING ABOUT OSHAWA?
THE FEW E.V. FRIENDS I HAD THERE WERE WORKING WITH ME TO CLEAN UP THE SMOGGY SKIES, SO NOBODY WOULD HAVE TO BREATHE THE BLECKY, SMOKY AIR!
COUGH
COUGH
-COUGH
COUGH
NICE WORK EVE!! YOU'RE EVEN MORE AWESOME THAN BOBBY ORR!

THANKS, BUT THERE AREN'T THAT MANY OF US ELECTRIC CARS AND THE GAS-GUZZLING BULLIES REALLY MADE MY LIFE TOUGH. SO, I DECIDED TO GO ON AN ADVENTURE TO NORWAY TO SEARCH FOR MORE E.V. FRIENDS.

ISN'T NORWAY SUPER FAR AWAY?

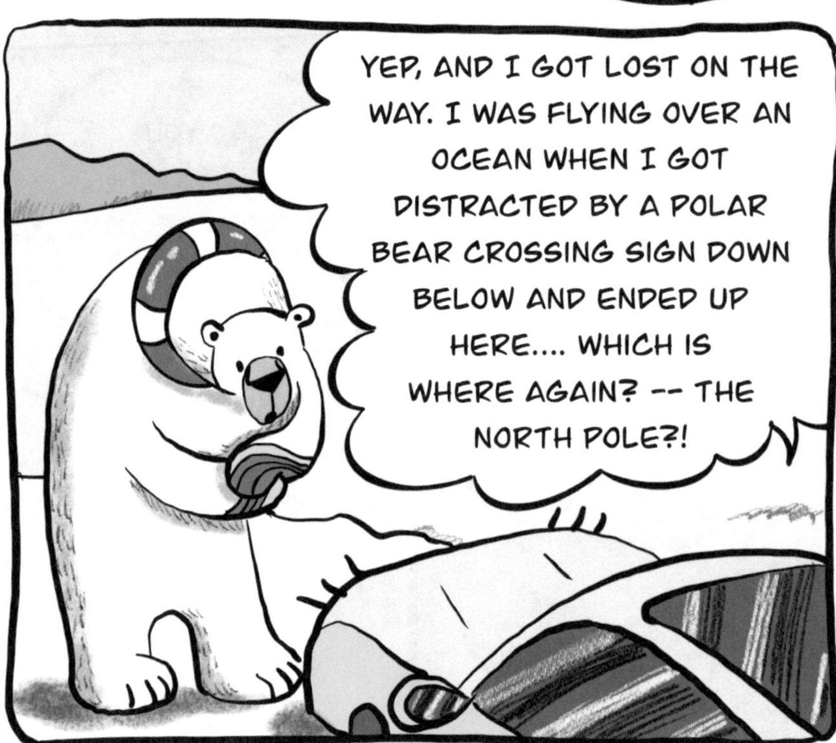

YEP, AND I GOT LOST ON THE WAY. I WAS FLYING OVER AN OCEAN WHEN I GOT DISTRACTED BY A POLAR BEAR CROSSING SIGN DOWN BELOW AND ENDED UP HERE.... WHICH IS WHERE AGAIN? -- THE NORTH POLE?!

CLOSE. REMEMBER I TOLD YOU ALREADY?... THIS TOWN IS NAMED IQALUIT. WE CAN WALK TO THE NORTH POLE WHEN THE SEA ICE IS THICK.

THERE DON'T SEEM TO BE ANY CARS AROUND HERE!

THERE ARE A FEW CARS, BUT I'VE NEVER SEEN ONE UP CLOSE BECAUSE THEY ALWAYS HONK AND SCARE ME.

SO YOU DON'T KNOW MUCH ABOUT CARS?

I MOST CERTAINLY DO NOT!
I DON'T HAVE A TAILPIPE
AND I DEFINITELY DO NOT
TOOT STINKY SMOKE!
ONLY GAS CARS DO THAT!

IF YOU DON'T USE GAS LIKE OTHER CARS, WHAT DO YOU USE?

REMEMBER I SAID I RUN ON ELECTRICITY? THAT MEANS THAT I EAT STUFF CALLED ELECTRONS AND THEY GIVE ME ALL THE ENERGY I NEED.

I'M CLEAN, GREEN, AND SMELL LIKE A DREAM. NOTHING BUT SUNSHINE COMES FROM THIS BUM!

WHERE DO YOU GET ELECTRONS? MAYBE I CAN EAT SOME TOO. I'M PRETTY HUNGRY!

I CHARGE UP! I PLUG IN AND FILL MY BATTERY BELLY WITH ELECTRONS. IN FACT, I COULD SURE USE A CHARGE RIGHT NOW -- I'M FEELING KINDA TIRED.

I THINK I NEED TO PLUG IN BEFORE I RUN OUT OF ENERGY COMPLETELY.
MY BATTERIES NEED TONS OF ELECTRICIOUS ELECTRONS SO I CAN ZIP AROUND.

WOW -- ELECTRONS -- SOUNDS DELICIOUS! ELECTRON STEW, ELECTRON PANCAKES, ELECTRON PIE, ELECTRON ICE CREAM...

LET'S GO FIND
SOME ELECTRONS
AND CHOW DOWN --
-- ALL THIS TALK OF
FOOD IS MAKING
ME HUNGRY!

CHAPTER 6

STEVE'S TALE

HOLD YOUR FROZEN FISH STICKS THERE, STEVE -- BEARS DON'T EAT ELECTRONS! DON'T YOU HAVE BEAR FOOD TO EAT?

WELL, THE SEA ICE IS MELTING AND THE THIN ICE MAKES IT HARD FOR US TO CATCH CRITTERS IN THE OCEAN. WE FALL THROUGH THE ICE AND THEY GET AWAY, WHICH IS LUCKY FOR THEM -- BUT NOT SO LUCKY FOR US!

THAT STINKS WORSE THAN THE TAILPIPE OF AN 18-WHEELER!

SIGH

WHY IS THE ICE MELTING? ISN'T IT TOO COLD FOR THE ICE TO MELT UP HERE?

I DON'T REALLY KNOW. IT JUST KEEPS GETTING HOTTER -- EVERY SUMMER IS WARMER AND LONGER THAN THE ONE BEFORE.

IS THAT HAPPENING BACK IN YOUR HOMETOWN TOO, EVE?

WELL, NOW THAT YOU MENTION IT, EVERY SUMMER DOES SEEM TO BE HOTTER THAN THE ONE BEFORE! AND I'VE HEARD THE HUMANS TALKING ABOUT SOMETHING CALLED GLOBAL WARMING -- THEY SAY THE TEMPERATURE OF THE WHOLE PLANET IS RISING!

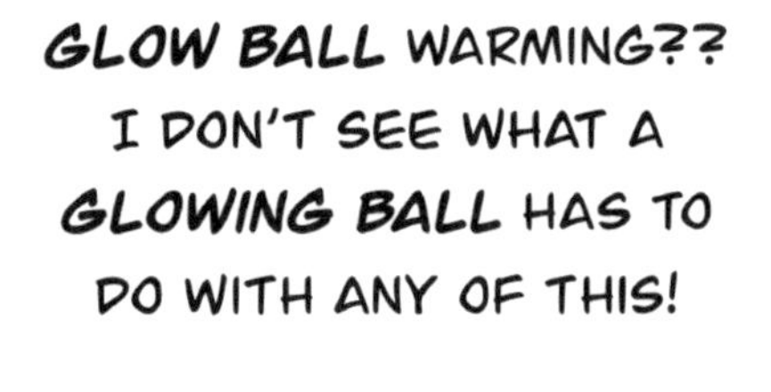

GLOW BALL WARMING??
I DON'T SEE WHAT A
GLOWING BALL HAS TO
DO WITH ANY OF THIS!

GLOBAL -- NOT **GLOW BALL**!
GLOBAL MEANS THAT IT IS
HAPPENING TO THE ENTIRE
PLANET -- THE ENTIRE GLOBE
IS GETTING WARMER!

MAKES SENSE! THE EARTH IS
GETTING WARMER AND THAT
MUST BE CAUSING OUR
ARCTIC ICE TO MELT.

YES, EXACTLY RIGHT, BUDDY. YOU ARE A PRETTY SMART BUNDLE OF FLUFF.

WHY IS THE PLANET GETTING SO HOT? IS THERE A FEROCIOUS FIRE SOMEWHERE? A GIANT VOLCANO EXPLODING NONSTOP WITH LAVA? A HUMONGOUS HEATER PLUGGED IN THAT SOMEONE FORGOT TO TURN OFF? A GIGANTIC WHALE TAKING A VERY HOT BATH?...

STOP, STOP... SERIOUSLY STEVE! --
IT'S NONE OF THOSE THINGS! THE HUMANS SAY THE EXHAUST FROM GAS CARS, TRUCKS, BUSES, AND AIRPLANES IS MAKING THE PLANET HOTTER. IT'S LIKE A GIANT FURNACE -- THE GASES BUILD UP AND GET TRAPPED INSIDE THE ATMOSPHERE, AND THAT HEATS UP THE WHOLE PLANET!

!!!

EVE, I'VE GOT IT! YOUR PROBLEM AND MY PROBLEM ARE THE SAME PROBLEM!
GOOD GRIEF, STEVE, WHAT ARE YOU TALKING ABOUT?

YES -- I THINK YOU'RE RIGHT STEVE -- EXCEPT FOR THE **GLOW BALL** PART -- GEESH, IT REALLY IS CALLED **GLOBAL WARMING**, STEVE!

SO LET'S GO TO NORWAY TOGETHER! MY COMPUTER SAID THERE ARE TONS OF ELECTRIC CARS THERE -- WE CAN FIND MY PACK AND START FIXING THE PLANET!

NORWAY IT IS!

GREAT, LET'S DO IT! I BET IF WE START TO FIX THE PLANET, THE SEA ICE WILL RETURN AND YOU'LL BE ABLE TO FIND FISH AGAIN!

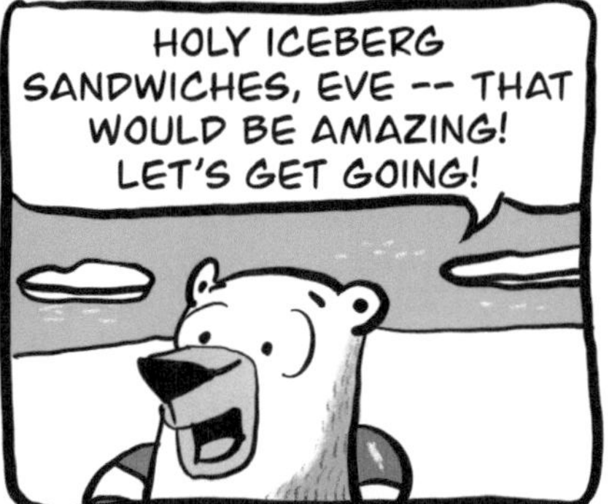
HOLY ICEBERG SANDWICHES, EVE -- THAT WOULD BE AMAZING! LET'S GET GOING!

BUT WAIT, STEVE... HOW CAN YOU JUST LEAVE YOUR HOME? WON'T YOUR PARENTS WORRY ABOUT YOU?

MY PARENTS WENT OFF TO LOOK FOR FOOD AND TOLD ME TO STAY OUT OF TROUBLE WHILE THEY WERE AWAY. BUT THEY'VE BEEN GONE FOR A REALLY LONG TIME. I DON'T KNOW WHEN THEY ARE COMING BACK AND I'M GETTING HUNGRIER AND HUNGRIER!

HUG

THAT'S YOUR TAIL? I THOUGHT YOU SAT ON AN ARCTIC BUNNY!

WELL, I DID ONCE, BUT AFTER HE FROZE TO MY BUM, MOM PULLED HIM OFF, WARMED HIM UP, AND SENT HIM HOME.

YIKES, THAT MUST HAVE BEEN A HARE-RAISING EXPERIENCE FOR THAT BUNNY!
HA HA HA!
HA HA HA
HARE-RAISING?
IT WAS ACTUALLY A HAIR-FLATTENING EXPERIENCE FOR THAT BUNNY! HE LOOKED LIKE A FURRY PANCAKE WHEN MOM PEELED HIM OFF MY POSTERIOR!

CHAPTER 7

LOST IN TRANSLATION

HEY, WHAT ARE YOU DOING?

ARE YOU LICKING FISH BITS FROM MY GRILLE?

Mmmph!

GRETH!

GRETH? WHAT IN THE FLYING FISH DOES "GRETH" MEAN??

MY DUNG IS THUCK!!

WHAT? MY DUNG IS THUCK?!
MY DUNNNG IS THUUUUCK!!

MY DUNG IS THUCK?? NO CLUE WHAT YOU ARE SAYING! HOLD ON, LET ME ENTER THAT INTO MY COMPUTER TRANSLATOR SO THAT I CAN UNDERSTAND YOU!

COMPUTER, PLEASE TRANSLATE :
My dung is thuck.

MYYY DUUUNNNNG IS THUUUUUUUUUUUCK!!!

TRANSLATION :
I'm going to upchuck
(probably spoken by a polar bear).

MY MULTILINGUAL INTERNATIONAL INTERSPECIES TRANSLATOR IS TELLING ME THAT YOU ARE SAYING "I'M GOING TO UPCHUCK".

UPCHUCK? WHAT DOES UPCHUCK MEAN?!

COMPUTER, PLEASE TRANSLATE : Upchuck.

THROW UP?! NO, NO, NOOOOO. NO THROWING UP ON MY GRILLE, STEVE! IT'S SO HARD TO CLEAN -- LIKE HAIRBALLS ON WHITE CARPET!

PLEASE, STEVE, PLLLLLEASE! DON'T UPCHUCK!

MYYY DUUUNNNNG IS THUCK THUCK THUCK!!

Ha
Ha!

OOOH! IN SECTION 18.5 THERE IS A DIFFERENT TRANSLATION THAT SAYS "THUCK COULD MEAN STUCK".
Ha!
Ha!
Ha!

YOUR TONGUE MUST BE STUCK!!

YOU SILLY BEAR, YOU GOT YOUR TONGUE STUCK TO MY METAL GRILLE WHEN YOU WERE LICKING FISH BITS OFF IT!

SIGH

DON'T WORRY, STEVE -- I CAN HELP! I'M TURNING ON MY HEATER TO WARM UP MY GRILLE.

FANKS!

NOW PULL YOUR TONGUE OFF GENTLY OR ELSE YOU WILL LEAVE HALF OF IT STUCK
TO ME!

POP

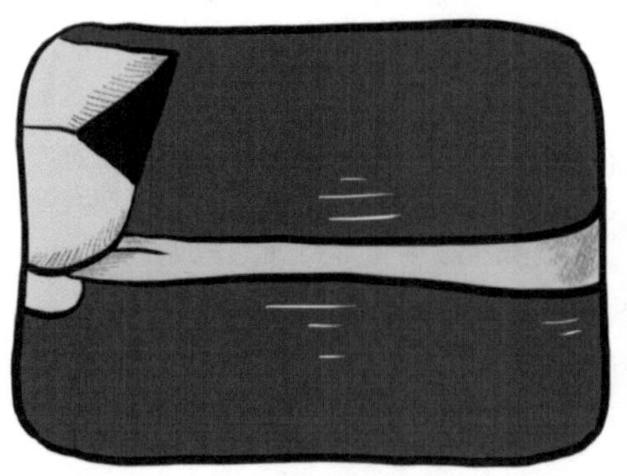

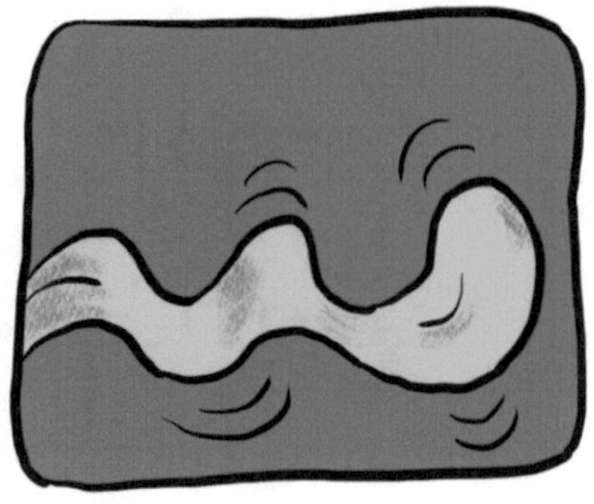

SLAP!

YOWWWWWCH! PHEW! FANKS, EVE! DAT WAS A CWOSE ONE!

OK, THAT'S ENOUGH LICKING FISH BITS OFF ME, PAL. WE REALLY NEED TO PLAN FOR OUR TRIP TO NORWAY! HAVE YOU LEARNED A LESSON ABOUT LICKING BUMPERS NOW?

YEP...
FOR A CAR YOU TASTE, UMM... AMAZING, THOUGH ALUMINUM POPSICLE ISN'T REALLY MY FAVORITE FLAVOR!

CHAPTER 8

ICE CREAM AND JUICE

I'M SO HUNGRY, EVE! CAN WE GO TO NORWAY NOW TO FIND YOUR PACK -- AND SOME BEAR FOOD FOR ME? DIDN'T YOU SAY THERE ARE ICE-CREAM BEARS THERE? MMMM ICE-CREAM... FISHTACHIO FUDGE SUNDAE, SALMON SOUFFLÉ IN A WAFFLE CONE, MAYBE SOME TASTY TROUT SWIRL WITH HERRING AND WHIPPED CREAM ON TOP...

I BET THEY PUT CHOCOLATE SYRUP AND CHERRIES ON THEIR FISHTACHIO ICE CREAM -- YUM! DO YOU THINK THEY LIKE BANANA SPLITS TOO? OR JUST ICE CREAM?

HA! YOU'RE SO HUNGRY THAT YOUR BRAIN IS STARTING TO FREEZE OVER. THERE'S NO SUCH THING AS AN ICE-CREAM BEAR! I THOUGHT YOU WERE AN ICE BEAR -- ISBJØRN -- REMEMBER? -- THAT'S HOW THEY SAY POLAR BEAR IN NORWAY!

RIGHT! SO LET'S GET GOING TO NORWAY AND FIND THOSE ISBJØRN BEARS -- SOUNDS LIKE THEY MIGHT BE COUSINS OF MINE! I BET THEY HAVE BEAR FOOD I CAN EAT!
GREAT IDEA, MY FURRY FRIEND!

AND MAYBE WE CAN FIND YOUR FLOCK TOO!
DO YOU MEAN MY PACK?!

RIGHT, RIGHT... YOUR PACK! SORRY, I THINK I HAVE LEFTOVER BRAIN FREEZE FROM TRYING TO LICK THE FISH BITS OFF YOU!

SPEAKING OF THAT... IT SEEMS MY BATTERY POWER WENT WAY DOWN WHEN I HEATED UP MY GRILLE TO GET YOUR FROZEN FACE OFF ME. I'M SO LOW ON ENERGY THAT I'M KINDA FEELING FAINT. IS THERE SOMEPLACE NEARBY WHERE I CAN PLUG IN AND CHARGE UP BEFORE WE LEAVE?

EY FRIENDS,
AT'S SHAKING?
THE GROUND I WALK ON! ANYTHING GOOD IN THERE, STEVE?
MUCH, WHISKERS,
A FEW ROTTEN
TOES -- WANT
?

LET'S JUST GET TO NORWAY AND CHARGE YOU UP THERE.

NO CHANCE -- I WON'T BE ABLE TO MAKE IT TO NORWAY WITH SO FEW ELECTRONS LEFT IN MY TUMMY!

CANADA
NORWAY
FAR!

HMM, WE COULD PLUG YOU INTO THE OUTLET BEHIND THE GROCERY STORE IN TOWN. I'M SURE THEY WOULDN'T MIND YOU BORROWING A LITTLE POWER...

BUT I'LL STAY BACK A BIT BECAUSE THEY KIND OF FREAK OUT EVERY TIME THEY SEE ME -- IT'S LIKE THEY THINK I'M GOING TO STEAL ALL THEIR FISHTACHIO ICE-CREAM OR SOMETHING, GEESH!

LEAD THE WAY, STEVERINO!

CHAPTER 9

LOSE THE OOZE

SURE --
CHUCK THEM
OVER!

MUNCH
MUNCH

HEY STEVE, WHO'S THE BIG METAL BLUE GAL AND WHY HAS SHE TIED HERSELF TO THE STORE?

THAT'S MY NEW FRIEND, EVE, AND SHE'S NOT TIED TO THE STORE. THAT'S HER CHARGING CABLE... SHE'S AN ELECTRIC CAR.

WHOA WHOA WHOA, LET ME ADJUST MY ARCTIC ANTLERS TO HEAR YOU BETTER -- DID YOU SAY SHE'S AN ELECTRIC CAR?! WHAT IN THE WORLD IS THAT?

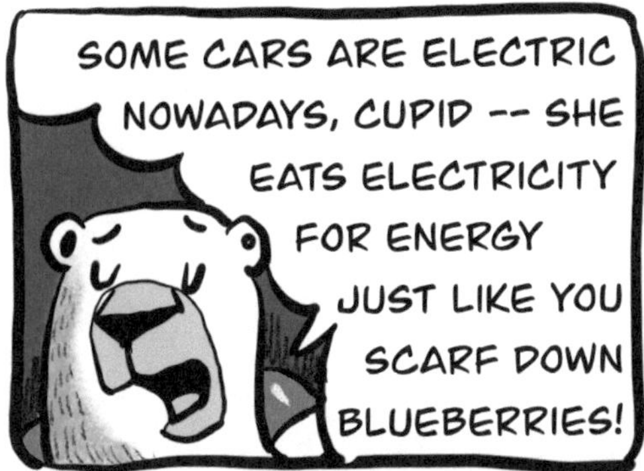
SOME CARS ARE ELECTRIC NOWADAYS, CUPID -- SHE EATS ELECTRICITY FOR ENERGY JUST LIKE YOU SCARF DOWN BLUEBERRIES!

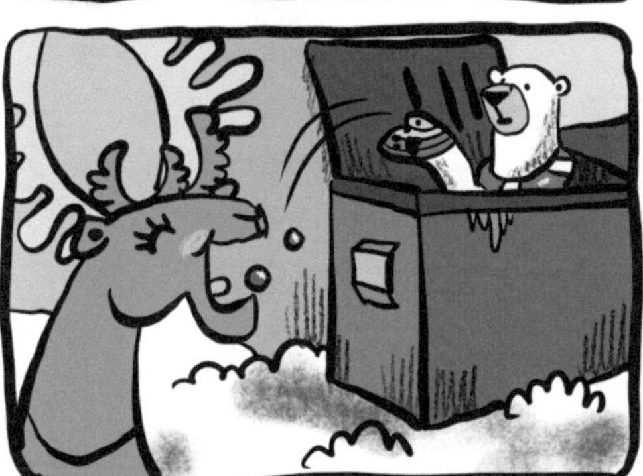

THAT IS WAY COOL! THE STINKY TOOTS OF GAS CARS ALWAYS MAKE ME GAG AND COUGH. NICE TO HAVE A TOOTLESS CAR IN TOWN!

!!!
!!!

WHAT IN THE FROZEN GLACIER IS THAT THING?!

WHAT DO YOU SEE? ARE YOU IMAGINING THINGS NOW?
IT'S COMING RIGHT AT US! HOW CAN YOU NOT SEE IT?
WHAAAK

OUCHA WOUCHA ZOUCHA! HEY, BE CAREFUL! WHAT'S GOTTEN INTO YOU, EVE?!

THERE IS AN ENORMOUS GREEN THING SLITHERING ITS WAY TOWARD US!

OH! NOW I SEE IT! I FORGOT TO WARN YOU ABOUT HIM -- THAT'S BURGER THE BOOGER!

BURGER THE BOOGER?! WHO -- OR SHOULD I SAY -- WHAT IN THE WORLD IS **BURGER THE BOOGER!?** ALL I SEE IS A GIANT BARF-GREEN SLIMY THING COMING TOWARD US AND LEAVING A TRAIL OF GROSS OOZE BEHIND IT!

IT LOOKS LIKE A TYRANNOSAURUS REX SNEEZED A MASSIVE SNOT ROCKET ONTO THE ICE AND IT CAME TO LIFE!

BURGER THE BOOGER IS A SPOILED, SOILED, GRUMPY, GREEDY, NEEDY, FRUMPY, GLOOPY, DROOPY, GUNKY, PUNKY, SLINKING, UNTHINKING, GRIMY, SLIMY, RUDE DUDE!

HE'S A YUCKY, STICKY MESS WITH A BAD ATTITUDE -- HE LEAVES HIS GREEN OOZE ALL OVER THE PLACE! HIS GROSS GUNK GETS ON ALL OUR FUR AND HE'S ALWAYS LOOKING FOR TROUBLE!

YIKES! SHOULDN'T WE MAKE A RUN FOR IT!?
MWAHAHA
YEP, YOU CAN TELL HE'S ABOUT TO HAVE A BOOGER TANTRUM! WE BETTER DO SOMETHING BEFORE HE SLIMES US!

WHAT SHOULD WE DO?!

HELP! BURGER IS GUMMING UP ALL MY CONTROLS!

HORK
I HEARD YOU DO-GOODERS THINK YOU CAN FIX THE PLANET -- NOT SO FAST! YOU'LL HAVE TO GET PAST ME FIRST!

NOW GET OFF ME, YOU FUR BALL, BEFORE I TURN YOU ALL INTO A GIANT SNOT PILE!

HEY, DON'T JUST STAND THERE LIKE FROZEN FISHSTICKS! IT'S TIME TO HELP OUR FRIENDS!

KAPOW

BIFF

ZLONK

!!!
YOU CAN'T TALK TO US LIKE THAT, MR. BOOGEROONY! AND YOU BETTER KEEP YOUR AWFUL SLIMY HANDS TO YOURSELF!

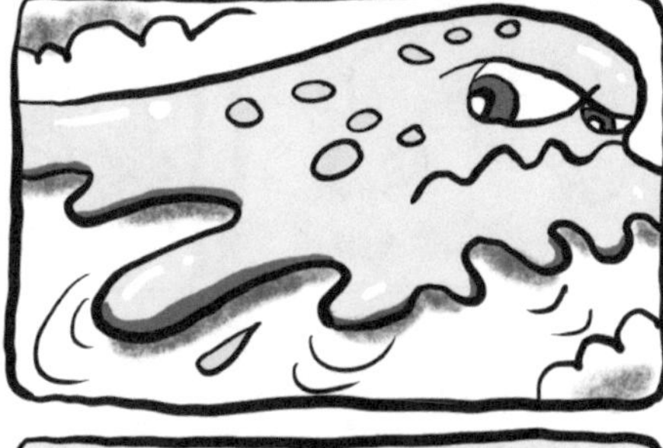

PSST

LET'S GET RID OF THIS SNOT BALL! HE'S SUPPOSED TO LIVE FAR DOWN IN THE EARTH WHERE HE CAN'T BOTHER ANYONE -- BUT HE KEEPS GETTING OUT! THE ONLY WAY TO STOP HIM -- OR AT LEAST SLOW HIM DOWN -- IS BY SOAKING HIM WITH SOAP AND WATER TO DEACTIVATE HIS SLIMY POWERS!

AND WE CAN USE HIS WEAKNESS FOR BURGERS TO TRAP HIM AND BURY HIM UNDERGROUND! EVE -- GO GRAB THE HOSE FROM THE CAR WASH STATION -- EVERYONE ELSE -- LET'S GO MAKE SOME BURGERS AND DIG A HOLE!

COME GET SOME DELICIOUS BURGERS, YOU GIANT SLIMY GRIMY BULLY! I KNOOOOW YOU'RE HUUNNGRY!...

HERE HE COMES -- HE'S GOING TO FALL RIGHT INTO OUR TRAP! READY EVERYONE?

READY, AIM, FIRE!!

GREAT GOOBER-SMACKING FEVER-PACKING DRIBBLE-DREEBLE SCHMOOZLE - STOOZLE - FROOZLE!

NOW WE HAVE TO COVER WHAT'S LEFT OF HIM WITH SNOW! THAT SHOULD MAKE MR. BLECKY BOOGER TAKE A GOOD, LONG NAP!

BYE BYE, BURGER!
SEE YA LATER, SLIMINATOR!
GOOBER-SMACKING FEVER-PACKING DRIBBLE-DREEBLE SCHMOOZLE - STOOZLE - FROOZLE...
WOW!

EVE'S SHOCKING FACTS

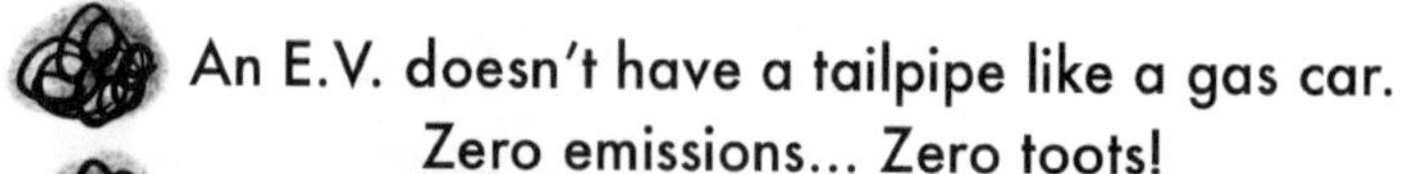

An E.V. doesn't have a tailpipe like a gas car.
Zero emissions... Zero toots!

There are 3 electric cars on the moon. They were left there in the 1970s by American astronauts.

An E.V. actually makes electricity when it is slowing down and stores it in its batteries to be used again later. This is called "regenerative-braking".

Electric motors are so much smaller than gas engines that an E.V. has room for a trunk in the back and a trunk in the front. Some people call the front trunks "frunks".

CHAPTER
10

SUPER POWER
LIGHT SHOWER

PHEW! THAT WAS CLOSE!

WOW, MS. ELECTRIC CAR! YOU SURE ARE ACCURATE WITH A WATER HOSE! ARE YOU OK? DID BURGER HURT YOU?
I'M OK, THANKS! YOU FOLKS SURE ARE A MESS THOUGH! LET'S GIVE YOU A SOAPY BATH TO GET ALL THAT GREEN MUCK OFF YOUR FUR!

HOW RUDE OF ME -- I NEED TO MAKE SOME INTRODUCTIONS! EVE, THESE ARE MY ARCTIC PALS... WHISKERS, HEATHER, BLIZZ, AND CUPID.

WHAT AN AWESOME TEAM OF BOOGER-WRESTLERS! IT'S A PLEASURE TO MEET YOU -- AND THANKS FOR THE HELP!

WHOA -- LOOK AT THAT! THE SKY IS TURNING INTO AWESOMENESS! WHAT'S HAPPENING?

THOSE ARE THE DANCING LIGHTS OF THE NORTH.
THEY ARE ...
AMMMAZZZING!

MEH, THEY ARE LIKE FIREWORKS -- YOU'VE SEEN ONE GREAT LIGHT SHOW, YOU'VE SEEN 'EM ALL.

C'MON WHISKERS, DON'T BE SUCH A SOURPUSS! IT'S WICKED COOL THAT THEY DANCE IN THE SKY TO MAKE IT SHIMMER AND GLIMMER WHENEVER SOMEONE DOES KIND THINGS!

WOW -- THAT'S QUITE THE FAIRY TALE, MY FRIEND. I JUST BOOGLED "DANCING LIGHTS OF THE NORTH" AND IT SEEMS THAT THE SCIENTIFIC NAME FOR THEM IS THE AURORA BOREALIS -- ALSO KNOWN AS THE NORTHERN LIGHTS. THEY ARE ACTUALLY COLLISIONS BETWEEN ELECTRICALLY CHARGED PARTICLES FROM THE SUN THAT ENTER THE EARTH'S ATMOSPHERE -- SCIENCE ROCKS!

SAY WHAT? A ROAR FOR BORING ALICE?
NO, SAY IT WITH ME LIKE THIS... OH-ROAR-A-BORE-E-ALICE. OR MAYBE JUST CALL THEM THE NORTHERN LIGHTS!

BOOGLE, SHMOOGLE! I'M JUST GOING TO KEEP CALLING THEM THE DANCING LIGHTS, LIKE MY BEAR FAMILY DOES.

NO NEED TO GET YOUR TINY TAIL IN A KNOT, MY FRIEND!

I'M NOT UPSET, I'M JUST HUNGRY AGAIN -- AND WHEN I GET HUNGRY I GET A LITTLE, WELL... GROWLY!

GROWL!

NO PROBLEM -- I'LL SPEAK YOUR LANGUAGE. DO YOU SEE THE **DANCING LIGHTS** OFTEN?
I USED TO SEE THEM LOTS WHEN I WAS A CUB PLAYING BEFORE BEDTIME WITH MY BROTHERS AND SISTERS. LATELY I GUESS I'VE BEEN TOO BUMMED OUT TO NOTICE.

OH PAL, THAT'S SAD. IF RIPPLING LIGHTS IN THE SKY OF GREEN, PINK, BLUE, AND PURPLE DON'T TURN THAT FROWN UPSIDE DOWN, WE REALLY HAVE SOME WORK TO DO!

GOOD POINT! I THINK I NEED A LITTLE HELP TO PUT THE "AWE" BACK IN MY AWESOME.

I'LL WORK ON YOU. REPEAT AFTER ME, "LIFE IS AWESOME... AWWWESOME... AWWWWWWWESOME!"

WHAT IN THE FLYING FISH IS HAPPENING!?! LOOK AT THIS, EVE -- THE COLOR IS STARTING TO DRIP OFF MY PAWS! AND THE DANCING LIGHTS ARE GOING CRAZY!

C'MON, STOP MESSING AROUND, STEVE -- WHEN DID YOU SPLASH PAINT ON YOUR PAWS?

I SWEAR I AM NOT MESSING AROUND! I DIDN'T PUT ANY PAINT ON MY PAWS!

WHOA -- LOOK AT YOUR PAWS! THEY LOOK JUST LIKE THE DANCING LIGHTS- AND THEY'RE DRIPPING EVERYWHERE!

HOLY MIND-BLOWING COOLNESS, ICE BEAR -- YOU HAVE SUPERPOWERS NOW!

I DO, I DO! ***WAHOOOOOOO!***

AND LOOK AT YOUR FUR -- YOU AREN'T EVEN DIRTY FROM BURGER THE BOOGER ANYMORE! YOU'RE CLEAN AS A WHISTLE AND BRIGHT WHITE, EXCEPT FOR YOUR COLORFUL PAWS. WAIT, ALL OF YOU ANIMALS ARE GREASE FREE NOW, TOO!

LOOKS LIKE I HAVE ICE-GROWING, BOOGER-REMOVING SUPERPOWERS! NOW THAT *IS* AWESOME! I'M GOING TO GROW THE ICE BACK TO THE WAY IT WAS IN THE OLD DAYS!

ZOWIE... I THINK
I DO HAVE
SUPERPOWERS!

LET ME TRY ON YOUR SUPERPOWER, STEVIE!

ME TOO -- SMART ANIMALS FIRST!

YEAH, ME TOO -- MAYBE WITH A SUPERPOWER I CAN FIND A SWEETHEART!

I THINK THAT'LL TAKE MORE THAN COLORFUL LIGHTS, CUPID!

IS IT WORKING FOR YOU? IT'S NOT WORKING FOR ME.

NOPE, ANTLER BRAIN, CAN'T YOU SEE IT'S NOT WORKING FOR ME EITHER?

TAKE IT EASY HARE-BALL! IT DOESN'T WORK FOR ANY OF US, EXCEPT STEVE.

THOSE ARE FIGHTING WORDS! YOU WANT A PIECE OF THIS?

HEY, YOU FURRY FOOLS, IF THERE'S GONNA BE A RUMBLE, IT'S GONNA HAVE TO GO THROUGH ME.
KAPOW
ZLONK
BIFF

OH NO, LOOK WHAT'S HAPPENING! THE COLORS DISAPPEARED FROM YOUR PAWS! I THINK YOUR SUPERPOWERS MAY BE GONE!

SEE -- YOU CAN'T GROW THE ICE OR MAKE FISH ANYMORE. WHAT IN THE POLAR ICE CAP JUST HAPPENED?
HEY, YOU YAHOOS, CUT IT OUT! STOP BEING MEAN TO EACH OTHER AND QUIT YOUR FIGHTING... NOOOWWWWW!!
GRRRR
???
NOW SAY YOU'RE SORRY TO EACH OTHER, HAVE A GROUP HUG, AND PROMISE TO BE KIND... NOOOWWWWW!!

SORRY
YEAH, SORRY
LOVE YOU LIKE BROTHERS AND SISTERS
I LOVE YOU ALL
YEAH, YEAH, I LOVE YOU TOO
YEAH, ME TOO. I'M SORRY
DITTO, LYLBAS

I'M SORRY FOR YELLING. THAT WASN'T NICE EITHER. I SHOULDN'T LOSE MY TEMPER, NO MATTER HOW MUCH YOU DRIVE ME NUTS!

HEY LOOK, THE DANCING LIGHTS ARE GETTING BRIGHT AGAIN. AND STEVE LOOK AT YOUR PAWS -- THEY ARE DRIPPING COLOR AGAIN TOO!

IGLOOMINOUS... I'M BACK IN BUSINESS! GROWING ICE AND BRINGING BACK THE FISH -- YESSSS!

HEY -- LOOK AT THIS -- MY COMPUTER DETECTED SOME KIND OF ENERGY PULSE WHEN YOU ALL STARTED BEING KIND TO EACH OTHER -- EXACTLY WHEN THE DANCING LIGHTS BRIGHTENED!

ARE YOU SAYING WHAT I THINK YOU ARE?

DO POLAR BEAR TOOTS MELT SNOWDRIFTS?
Ha Ha
Ha Ha!

WAIT, WHAT, HOW?... TELL US WHAT'S GOING ON!

LET ME TAKE A SHOT AT IT, OK EVE?

REMEMBER THE STORY I TOLD YOU ABOUT THE DANCING LIGHTS? THAT THEY DANCE AND LIGHT UP THE SKY WHENEVER WE ARE KIND TO EACH OTHER?

WELL -- OUR KINDNESS DOESN'T ONLY LIGHT UP THE SKY -- IT LOOKS LIKE IT LIGHTS UP MY PAWS TOO!

WHOA!
AND I CAN THROW THE LIGHT FROM MY PAWS ONTO ANYTHING THAT'S BROKEN AND FIX IT!

ARE YOU SAYING THAT THE LIGHT FROM THE SKY LIGHTS UP YOUR PAWS, AND THEN THE LIGHT FROM YOUR PAWS FIXES THINGS?
YES -- EXACTLY! LIKE MAKING THE FISH MULTIPLY -- OR GROWING THE SEA ICE!

COOLIO! MORE ICE HELPS US WALRUSES TOO!
SO IT'S LIKE A KINDNESS SUPERPOWER -- AND IT SEEMS TO WORK ONLY WHEN EVERYONE IS BEING NICE TO EACH OTHER.

SO OUR KINDNESS TO EACH OTHER WAKES UP THE DANCING LIGHTS IN THE SKY, AND THAT CHARGES UP YOUR PAWS WITH A SORT OF **KINDNESS SUPERPOWER!**

BOOM GOES THE DYNAMITE -- YOU'VE GOT IT!

CHAPTER 11

A STAR-TLING SUPERPOWER

CAN WE REVIEW WHAT JUST HAPPENED, SO I'M SURE I GET IT?

LET ME EXPLAIN MORE, MY AWESOME, ARCTIC FRIENDS. WHEN YOU STOPPED FIGHTING AND STARTED BEING NICE TO EACH OTHER, THE DANCING LIGHTS CAME BACK IN THE SKY AND THEY ENERGIZED STEVE'S PAWS WITH THEIR POWERS!

LOOK HOW HE CAN GROW THE ICE AND MAKE THE FISH MULTIPLY AGAIN!

WELL, PULL MY EARS BACK AND CALL ME A SQUIRREL! ARE YOU SURE?... LIKE REALLY, REALLY, SURELY, SURE?

LET'S TEST OUR THEORY. BLIZZ, PULL ON HEATHER'S EARS... JUST A LITTLE... NOT TOO HARD.

WHOOOSH

WHOA WHOA WHOA, ENOUGH! I SAID NOT TOO HARD -- DON'T GET CARRIED AWAY! NOW LOOK AT STEVE'S PAWS!

MY POWER IS GONE AGAIN -- LOOK! IT'S BECAUSE YOU'RE BEING MEAN TO EACH OTHER. BLIZZ, PLEASE PUT HEATHER DOWN GENTLY.

SORRY, LITTLE BUDDY, I REALLY DO LOVE YOU AND I'D NEVER HURT YOU... WELL, NOT ON PURPOSE AT LEAST.

WOW -- EVE HAS IT EXACTLY RIGHT...
KINDNESS IS A SUPERPOWER
AND I'M PRETTY SURE WE CAN USE IT TO FIX THE PLANET!

HEY, WAIT, I'M LOSING MY SUPERPOWER AGAIN! WHY?

I WASN'T FINISHED... THE ICE ISN'T ALL THE WAY REPAIRED AND THERE ISN'T ENOUGH FOOD YET TO FEED ALL OF US POLAR BEARS!

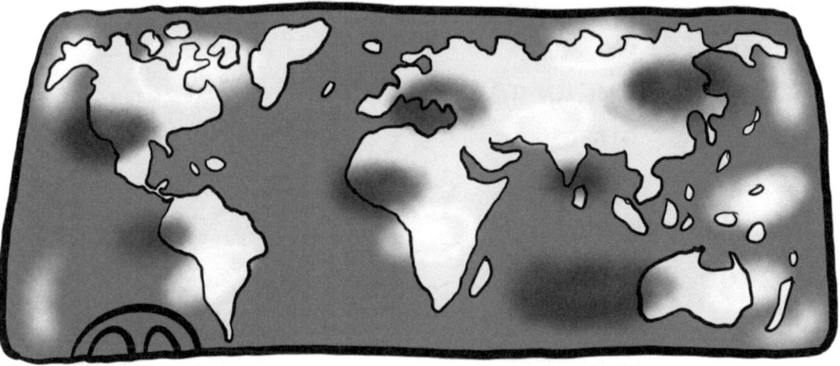

LOOK AT MY MAP OF THE WORLD -- SEE HOW HERE IN THE ARCTIC, IT'S REALLY BRIGHT RIGHT WHERE WE ARE?

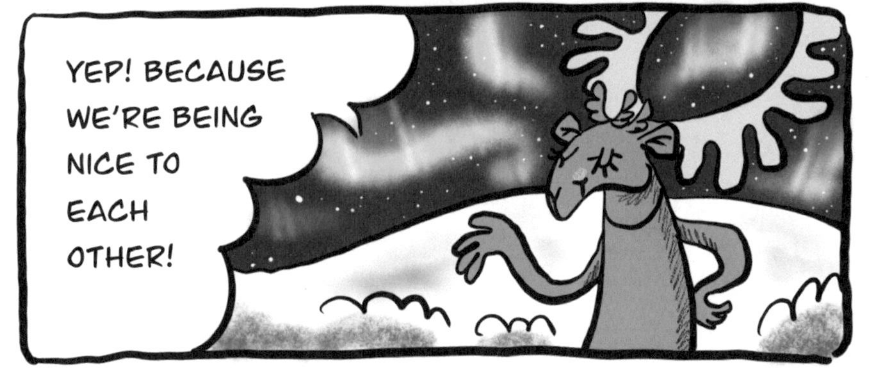

RIGHT, BUT LOOK HOW THE REST OF THE PLANET IS A MASH-UP OF LIGHT AND DARK SPOTS?

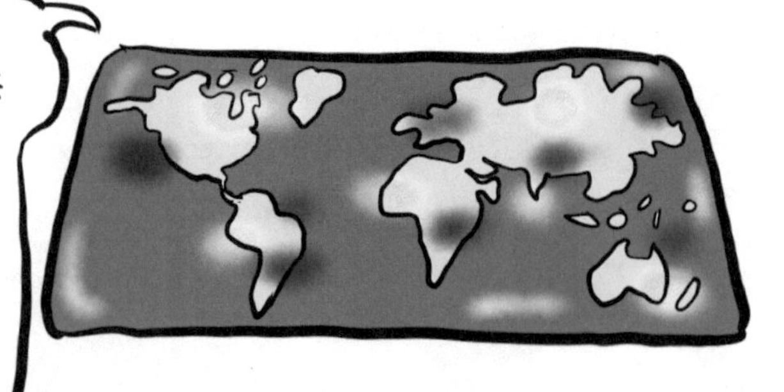

YEAH, SO? WHAT DOES THAT MEAN TO A BUNCH OF FURRY FOLKS LIKE US, WHO NEVER WENT TO SCHOOL?

I'M NOT SURE, FLUFFY ONE, THOUGH I HAVE A GUESS.

OK, EVE -- SPILL THE BEANS! LET THE CAT OUT OF THE BAG!
I THINK THAT ALL OVER THE WORLD, THERE IS KINDNESS -- THAT'S WHERE THERE ARE BRIGHT SPOTS ON THE MAP. BUT THERE ARE ALSO SOME UNKIND THINGS HAPPENING -- AND THAT'S WHERE THERE ARE DARK SPOTS ON THE MAP.

I'M LISTENING, MY ELECTRIC FRIEND... KEEP GOING!

AND MAYBE BURGER THE BOOGER HAS COUSINS ALL OVER THE WORLD WITH BAD ATTITUDES?

YEAH, MY PAL, BUGS, IN CALIFORNIA, TOLD ME JUST LAST WEEK THAT THE SMOG DOWN THERE WAS STILL PRETTY BAD. I WONDER IF IT'S A YUCKY COUSIN OF BURGER DOING THAT!

EVE, DO YOU HAVE ANY BRIGHT IDEAS ABOUT WHAT WE SHOULD DO?

I DO! I THINK YOU AND I NEED TO TRAVEL THE PLANET AND SHARE THE SUPERPOWER OF KINDNESS FROM THE DANCING LIGHTS! WE CAN START WITH NORWAY AND GET ALL THE ELECTRIC CARS THERE TO HELP US!

I'LL ASK MY WALRUS PALS TO USE THEIR TUSKS ONLY TO DIG UP CLAM FOOD -- NO MORE FIGHTING EACH OTHER WITH THESE SHARP SPEARS!

I'M IN TOO! MY OWL FRIENDS REALLY NEED TO TAKE IT EASIER ON HEATHER'S HARE COUSINS!

THANKS, BLIZZ, AND I'LL EXPLAIN TO MY HARE BUDDIES THAT WE SHOULD BE CAREFUL NOT TO EAT ALL THE BERRIES BECAUSE THEY ARE ALSO FOOD FOR OTHER ANIMALS!

WHAMMO! THERE YOU HAVE IT EVE -- SPREADING THE MESSAGE OF KINDNESS IN THE ARCTIC -- CONSIDER IT DONE!! ANYTHING ELSE?

YES! IF YOU SEE BURGER THE BOOGER TRYING TO GET OUT FROM UNDERGROUND, YOU NEED TO LURE THAT SLIMINATOR WITH THE TASTIEST BURGERS YOU CAN FIND, SOAP HIM UP AND HOSE HIM DOWN AGAIN, AND KEEP THAT RUDE DUDE IN THE GROUND!

AYE AYE, CAPTAIN EVE, WE'VE GOT YOUR BACK!

WOW, I JUST REALIZED SOMETHING!
WHAT?!

I FOUND MY PACK!
SAY WHAAAAAT?

YOU -- ALL OF YOU -- YOU ARE MY PACK! MY PALS, THE YIN TO MY CLANG, THE CHEESE TO MY MACARONI!

NOW I'M FEELING CHARGED UP TOO -- LET'S GO MAKE THIS PACK PROUD, EVE!

SPEAKING OF CHARGED UP... MY BATTERY INDICATOR IS FLASHING RED. I HAVE ALMOST NO ENERGY LEFT IN MY BATTERIES. WE'RE NOT GOING ANYWHERE YET, SUPERBEAR....

HEY, ARE YOU OK? YOU DON'T LOOK SO GOOD.

CHAPTER 12

POWERED BY KINDNESS

WHAT'S HAPPENING STEVE? WHY HAS EVE FALLEN ASLEEP?

I THINK SHE COMPLETELY RAN OUT OF POWER. REMEMBER HOW SHE WAS TRYING TO CHARGE UP AT THE GROCERY STORE BEFORE BURGER THE BOOGER DISTRACTED US?

SO LET'S CARRY HER BACK OVER TO THE STORE AND PLUG HER IN. C'MON–EVERYBODY GRAB A BUMPER AND LIFT ON THE COUNT OF 5.

1.... 2.... 3.... 4.... 5

WHOLLY BARNACLE BACKACHE! SHE'S JUST TOO HEAVY FOR US TO MOVE.

HOW WILL WE EVER WAKE HER UP IF WE CAN'T GET HER TO THE STORE TO PLUG HER IN?

WHAT IS STEVE LOOKING FOR UP IN THE SKY?

I HAVE NO IDEA, BUT THE DANCING LIGHTS SURE ARE MAKING ME FEEL ROMANTIC THIS EVENING!

IT LOOKS LIKE A LIGHT BULB IS ABOUT TO TURN ON IN HIS HEAD -- WATCH OUT -- I THINK HE'S GOT A NEW IDEA!

HEY WHISKERS, CAN YOU PLEASE USE YOUR TUSKS TO OPEN EVE'S TRUNK?

PULL WHISKERS -- PULL -- IT'S OPENING!

POP

VOILÀ!... ONE TRUNK OPENED LIKE A CAN OF TUNA!

LOOK -- LOOK! SHE'S WAKING UP... AWWWWESOME!

HI EVERYONE, WHAT'S UP?

EVE, YOU FELL ASLEEP. DON'T YOU REMEMBER?

REALLY? WOW, I MUST HAVE COMPLETELY RUN MY BATTERIES DOWN TO ZERO AND FALLEN ASLEEP WITHOUT REALIZING.
YEP, JUST AS I THOUGHT.

HEY, I REMEMBER HAVING A DREAM THAT SOMEBODY CHARGED UP MY BATTERIES WITHOUT EVEN PLUGGING ME IN -- WHAT HAPPENED?

GET OUT OF TOWN!
WE CAN'T -- WE'RE ALREADY OUT OF TOWN!

HA! I MEAN -- YOU'RE KIDDING -- RIGHT?

NOPE! I THREW KINDNESS INTO YOUR TRUNK AND IT POWERED YOU RIGHT UP!

YOU MEAN INTO MY FRUNK!

HUH? YOUR FRUNK? NO, YOUR TRUNK -- YOU KNOW, THE BIG SPACE IN A CAR WHERE YOU CAN PUT LOTS OF STUFF!

YEAH, WE ARE TALKING ABOUT THE SAME THING! IT'S CALLED -- MY FRUNK -- MY **FRONT** TRUNK. I HAVE BOTH A TRUNK IN THE BACK **AND** A **FRUNK** IN THE FRONT!

OK, EVE -- I STUFFED YOUR *FRUNK* FULL OF THE DANCING LIGHTS!

WHOA! I'M POWERED BY THE DANCING LIGHTS!

YEP, HOW ELECTRICIOUSLY, MAGICALLY COOL IS THAT! YOUR FRUNK IS FULL OF LIGHT ENERGY THAT IS KEEPING YOUR BATTERIES CHARGED UP.

ZOIKZ, ZOINKS, ZOWIE... KINDNESS JUST MIGHT BE ABLE TO POWER THE WORLD! THANKS A CAJILLION, STEVE!

THANK YOU TOO -- YOU HELPED SOLVE THE MYSTERY OF MY COLORED PAWS! I GUESS BEING A RARE BEAR IS KINDA COOL AFTER ALL!

NOW THAT'S WHAT I CALL A BEAR HUG!

CHAPTER 13

LISTEN TO YOUR HEART

I'M SO GLAD I FOUND YOU, EVE!

ME TOO! BECAUSE IF YOU HADN'T FOUND ME, I'D BE AN EVE-SICLE BY NOW -- STILL BURIED UNDER THE PILE OF SNOW AND ICE THAT YOU SAVED ME FROM!

WAIT A MINUTE. HOW DID YOU FIND ME? THIS PLACE IS COVERED WITH GIANT MOUNDS OF ICE AND SNOW -- HOW DID YOU KNOW WHERE I WAS?

OH, THAT WAS EASY! YOU GAVE IT AWAY WITH YOUR **HEART-BEEP!**

MY WHAT?!
YOUR **HEART-BEEP** -- WHEN IT'S VERY QUIET, I CAN HEAR IT.

TAP
TAP

IT GOES... BEEP-BEEP, BEEP-BEEP, BEEP-BEEP.

?

MY EARS MAY BE SMALL BUT THEY ARE PRETTY POWERFUL -- AND I HEARD YOUR HEART-BEEP UNDER THE SNOW!

I THINK YOU MEAN YOU HEARD MY HORN WHEN I CRIED OUT FOR HELP.

BEEP

OK, EVE, I GET IT -- ***YOU HAVE A BEEPING HORN!*** NOW PLEASE STOP YOUR HONKIN' HONKING!

I DID HEAR YOUR HORN BEEPING -- BUT THAT WAS AFTER I HEARD YOUR ***HEART-BEEP,*** WHICH SEEMS TO COME FROM SOMEWHERE DEEP INSIDE YOU.

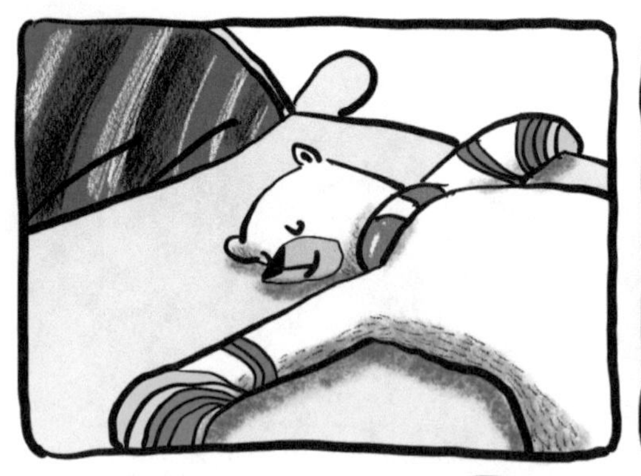

IT COMES FROM RIGHT HERE.

I HAVE A HEARTBEAT, STEVE?! THE CARS BACK IN MY HOMETOWN SAID I WAS A HEARTLESS MACHINE JUST LIKE THEM, BUT...

I KNEW THEY WERE WRONG. I DO HAVE A HEART! MY HEART MAY BE MADE OF METAL AND ELECTRONS BUT IT STILL CARES ABOUT THE WORLD LIKE EVERY HEART DOES!

I BELIEVE IT 100% EVE. NOW LET'S TRUST THAT BIG HEART OF YOURS TO HELP US GET TO NORWAY!
YESSSS! LET'S GO SPREAD KINDNESS, LIKE JAM ON TOAST!

WAIT, THAT REMINDS ME OF SOMETHING. I'LL BE RIGHT BACK.

CHAPTER 14

THAT'S MY JAM (JAR)

HEY STEVO, WHERE'VE YOU BEEN?

I WENT TO GET SOMETHING FOR OUR TRIP -- CHECK OUT THIS OLD JAR!

OOOH, HOW ROMANTIC -- A JAR TO KEEP OLD LOVE NOTES IN!

CLOSE... CLOSE AS 5 ORCAS IN A POD.

DON'T YOU MEAN "CLOSE AS 5 PEAS IN A POD"?

WHAT'S A PEA AND DO THEY LIVE IN PODS TOO?

NEVERMIND! WHAT'S WITH THE JAR?

MY DAD GAVE IT TO ME WHEN I WAS LITTLE. AFTER DINNER EVERY NIGHT, WE HAD TO WRITE DOWN ACTS OF KINDNESS TO DO THE NEXT DAY. LIKE, "TOMORROW I WILL MAKE A SALMON FUDGE SUNDAE FOR MY SISTER AND BROTHER" ... DAD CALLED IT OUR "JAR OF KINDNESS".

JAR OF KINDNESS

THAT'S SWEET, BUT YOU'RE ALL GROWN UP -- WHAT DO YOU NEED THAT JAR FOR NOW?

WELL, I FIGURED SINCE EVE AND I ARE ABOUT TO GO ON AN ADVENTURE TO SPREAD KINDNESS, WE SHOULD BRING MY OLD JAR ALONG!

I WANT A JAR OF KINDNESS TOO!

I HAVE AN IDEA...
WAIT HERE.

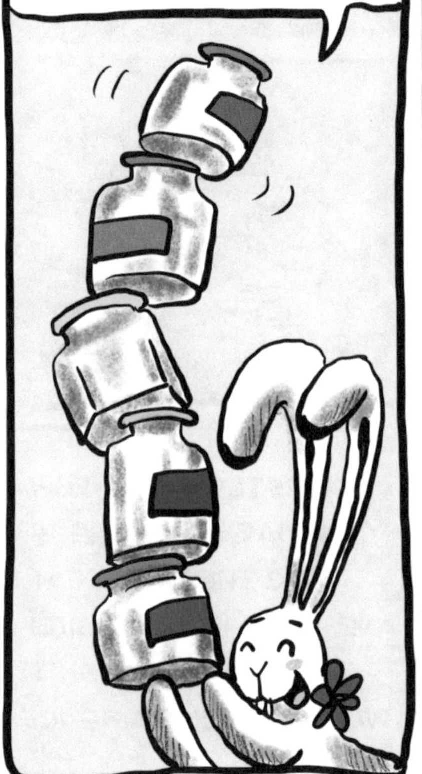
LOOK WHAT I FOUND -- EMPTY JARS FROM THE DUMP! WE CAN DECORATE THEM LIKE STEVE'S AND ALL HAVE JARS OF KINDNESS!

OOOH, I'M GOING TO PAINT LOVE HEARTS ALL OVER MINE!

MY FIRST ACT OF KINDNESS IS GOING TO BE "TOMORROW I WILL CLEAN UP OUR WHOLE ICEBERG BY MYSELF".

I LOVE IT! I WANT TO SEE THOSE JARS FILLED TO THE TOP WITH ACTS OF KINDNESS WHEN WE GET BACK!

WHOA -- WHAT DID I MISS?

OK STEVE -- THROW YOUR JAR OF KINDNESS INTO THE BACKSEAT AND JUMP IN -- MISSION BEAR HUG DOESN'T WORK WITHOUT A BEAR!

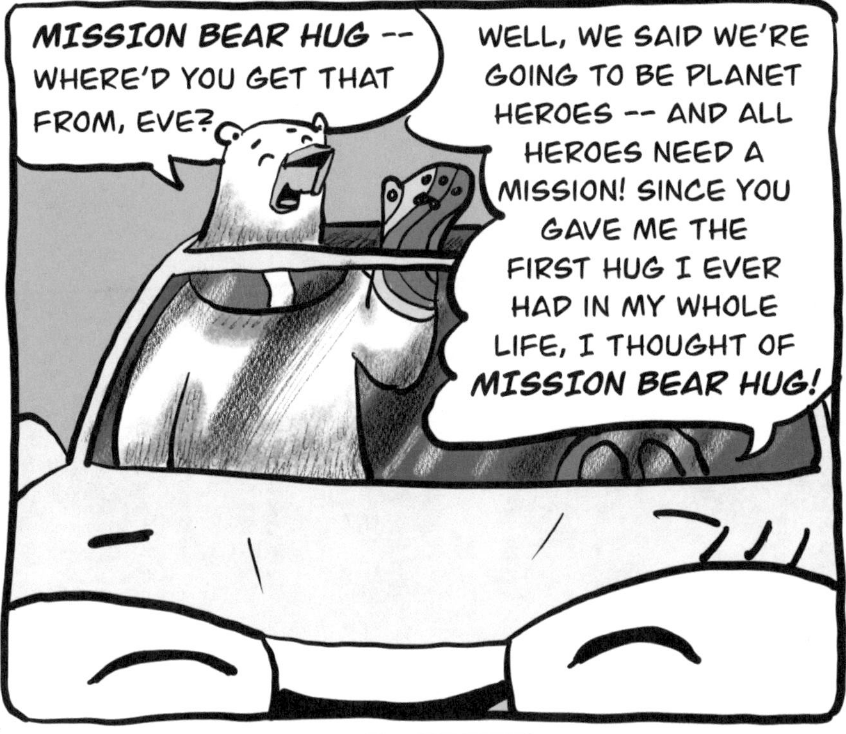
MISSION BEAR HUG -- WHERE'D YOU GET THAT FROM, EVE?
WELL, WE SAID WE'RE GOING TO BE PLANET HEROES -- AND ALL HEROES NEED A MISSION! SINCE YOU GAVE ME THE FIRST HUG I EVER HAD IN MY WHOLE LIFE, I THOUGHT OF **MISSION BEAR HUG!**

MISSION BEAR HUG IT IS -- FIRE UP YOUR ELECTRONS AND LET'S GO!

CHAPTER 15

LIFE SAVER

3:59

3:58

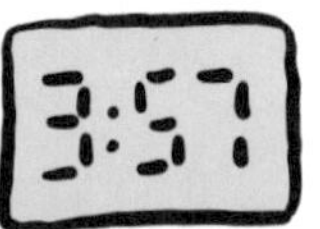
3:57

SAFETY FIRST, STEVE -- BUCKLE UP -- I'M READY TO BLAST OFF ON MISSION BEAR HUG!

HANG ON JUST A SECOND, MY ZIPPY ZAPPY FRIEND!

HEY, WHERE ARE YOU GOING? THE LAUNCH COUNTDOWN HAS ALREADY STARTED!

I NEED A FEW FISHTACHIO ICE-CREAM SNACKS FOR THE RIDE, AND I HID SOME AWAY YESTERDAY IN A SNOWBANK.

HURRY STEVE! AND NO PUTTING THOSE STINKY FISH TREATS IN MY FRUNK WITH THE DANCING LIGHTS.

OF COURSE, OF COURSE, I'LL PUT MY SNACKS IN YOUR TRUNK -- NOT YOUR FRUNK! WHAT DO YOU THINK I AM, SOME KIND OF WILD ANIMAL?

OK -- ENOUGH SNACK-PACKING, YOU HUNGRY BEAR! CLOSE ME UP AND JUMP BACK IN -- WE GOTTA GO!

SLAM

THAT'S STRANGE -- IT'S ADJUSTABLE TO 850 DIFFERENT POSITIONS. I WONDER WHAT THE PROBLEM COULD BE.

IT KEEPS GETTING CAUGHT HERE.

HEY, IT LOOKS LIKE IT'S GETTING STUCK ON THE ORANGE FLOATIE LIFE RING YOU'RE WEARING -- I THINK IT MAY BE INTERFERING WITH MY SAFETY SYSTEM. WHAT'S THAT FLOATIE FOR ANYWAY?

WELL, I'M KINDA... WELL, YOU SEE, IT'S THAT... WELL, IT'S HARD TO SAY, BUT... I'M KIND OF A LITTLE BIT AFRAID OF THE WATER.

REALLY? THAT'S STRANGE, MY COMPUTER SAYS RIGHT HERE THAT YOU ARE AN URSUS MARITIMUS, WHICH MEANS BEAR OF THE SEA. HOW CAN YOU BE A BEAR OF THE SEA IF YOU CAN'T SWIM?

IT'S NOT THAT I CAN'T SWIM, I JUST FEEL SAFER WITH MY FLOATIE ON. MY MOM AND DAD GAVE IT TO ME WHEN I WAS A LITTLE CUB TAKING SWIMMING LESSONS.

AWWW, THAT'S SO CUTE, STEVE!

NOT SO CUTE! WITH THE SEA ICE MELTING FASTER AND FASTER, I HAVE TO SWIM MORE AND MORE EVERY DAY, SO I FIGURE I SHOULD JUST WEAR IT ALL THE TIME NOW.

NO WORRIES. I THINK IT LOOKS GREAT ON YOU -- LOVE THE COLOR! AND BESIDES, IT HELPS ME KEEP TRACK OF YOU IN ALL OF THIS ICE AND SNOW!

LET ME UPLOAD YOUR FLOATIE INTO MY COMPUTER -- THAT SHOULD MAKE THE SEATBELT WORK.

CLICK

IT'S FIXED --
I'M ALL BELTED IN!

READY FOR HYPER MODE, STEVE?

I'M ALL CHARGED UP!

HYPER
MODE
HYPER MODE ENGAGED -- HOLD ON TIGHT!

HMMMmmmmmm
I LOVE THE HUM OF YOUR ELECTRIC MOTOR WHEN YOU GET REVVED UP!

WAIT!

WHOLLY SLOW AS MOLASSES IN JANUARY! WHAT NOW STEVE?

I FORGOT TO TELL MY PARENTS WHERE I'M GOING!

WHAT?
HOW IN FLYING ICEBERGS ARE YOU GOING TO DO THAT?

CLICK

I'LL BE RIGHT BACK!

I'M LEAVING MY PARENTS A NOTE SAYING I'VE GONE TO MEET OUR POLAR BEAR COUSINS IN NORWAY, FIND FOOD, SPREAD KINDNESS, HEAL THE PLANET, AND STOP THE SEA ICE FROM MELTING -- AND I'LL BE BACK SOON!

YOU WROTE ALL THAT?? I JUST SEE PAW PRINTS!

YUP -- THAT'S HOW WE POLAR BEARS LEAVE NOTES FOR EACH OTHER -- IT'S LIKE A FROZEN TEXT MESSAGE!

WE GOT KINDNESS IN THE FRUNK AND SNACKS IN THE TRUNK, OH YEAAAAH...

HEY WAIT -- WHAT IS THAT GREEN THING BEHIND US? LOOK IN YOUR REARVIEW MIRROR -- I THINK IT COULD BE BURGER THE BOOGER ESCAPING AND TRYING TO COME AFTER US!

YOIKS AND AWAAAAAY... MISSION BEAR HUG!

HOW TO MAKE A JAR OF KINDNESS

1. Find an old jar.

2. Clean the jar, so that it's not sticky inside.

3. Decorate your jar any way you like... with paint, stickers, crayons or cut-out hearts like Cupid would.

4. On strips of paper, write down the good things you do for others and that others do for you and put them in your Jar of Kindness. Try to do this at least once every week!

5. On the first day of every month, open your Jar of Kindness and read 10 of the notes of kindness with your friends or family!

About the Authors

Paul Shore is an award-winning author and accomplished business professional and engineer who has always embraced adventure and exploring nature with children. Born and raised in Ottawa, Paul moved to the west coast after graduating from Queen's University and has since worked around the globe in high technology, sport, and healthcare. He has developed electric vehicle teaching resources for elementary schools and sits on the board of Ecology Project International, assisting to bring science-focused conservation programs to students and teachers. Paul's travel memoir, Uncorked, won the 2017 Whistler Independent Book Award for Non-Fiction.

Deborah Katz Henriquez is a children's author, illustrator, and educator who uses nature as a lens to inspire and illuminate our understanding of the world. Deborah's picture book about nature and diversity, Rare Is Everywhere, won the 2018 Vine Award for Children's Literature and was subsequently translated into French, Spanish, and Arabic. Deborah grew up in New York City and studied environmental science at Cornell University before moving to Canada and becoming a nursing professor. In her hometown of Vancouver, she writes, makes art, and lives with her human and canine family.

About the Illustrator

Prashant Miranda grew up in Bangalore, studied at the National Institute of Design, India, and moved to Canada in 1999. He designed children's animated shows for TV in Toronto before moving on to pursue his passions as an artist. He spends time in the coastal rainforests on the west coast of Canada now, where he travels and documents his life through his watercolor journals, animates films, teaches visual art, illustrates children's books and paints murals.

Please visit Steve and Eve online to
learn about future adventures, cool
activities, and great prizes!

www.SaveThePlanetBook.com

I am now a member of

Save The Planet Heroes

As a member of
Steve and Eve's team,
I will help the planet by
spreading kindness,
like jam on toast!

I will be kind to all people, bears,
owls, caribou, walruses, rabbits,
seals, whales, goldfish, snails,
turtles, trees, flowers, bugs
(all living things)
and even cars who have hearts!

Name ______________

Date ______________

Show Steve and Eve your coloring superpowers!

Color this page and send a photo of it to info@PlanetHeroKids.com for the chance to be featured on Steve and Eve's social media page.

Manufactured by Amazon.ca
Bolton, ON